T5-CQD-793

A faint smile crossed Kurt's face as his fingers idly traced the outline of the keys through his graduation gown. They were more than just keys to a car and a cabin. They were keys to life and the future. He was graduating from high school, but he wanted this night to be something more than that. He wanted it to be the beginning of a new world of experience—a commencement to life.

GRADUATION WEEKEND

Ed Groenhoff

ACCENT BOOKS
Denver, Colorado 80215

ACCENT BOOKS

A division of Accent Publications, Inc.
12100 W. Sixth Avenue
P.O. Box 15337
Denver, Colorado 80215

Copyright©1985 Accent Publications, Inc.
Printed in the United States of America

All rights reserved. No portion of this book may be reproduced
in any form without the written permission of the publishers,
with the exception of brief excerpts in magazine reviews.

Library of Congress Catalog Card Number 84-072314
ISBN 0-89636-149-7

To Tim

Contents

Graduation or Commencement?

Kurt could feel the keys in his pocket even through the graduation gown. A faint smile crossed his face as his fingers idly traced the outline of the keys on the red fabric. They were more than just keys to a car and a cabin. They were keys to life and the future. He was graduating from high school, but he wanted this night to be something more than that. He wanted it to be the beginning of a new world of experience— a commencement to life.

The speaker was on point four and seemed to be nearing a conclusion. Kurt glanced up and down the row of red-robed seniors on either side of him. It was obvious that few were listening, and Kurt wondered how many were going over the details of the night ahead rather than listening to the speaker.

After what seemed like hours, Kurt heard those magic words, "In conclusion," and he straightened up in his chair. He remembered a few words from the speech—words like "potential," "challenge," and "future"—words he had heard many times in the past few weeks. It seemed that every graduation card contained one or more of them, and every adult used at least one of them when talking to him about his graduation.

He tried to see Terri's face, but she was sitting across the aisle and ahead of him, so all he could see was her long dark-brown hair flowing from under her mortarboard. He wondered what she was thinking, and if she was looking forward to the night ahead. She was his date for the all-night graduation party, and she had promised to come with an answer to a very important question. Neither of them could know, at this moment, that the course of their lives would be dramatically altered before morning.

The speech was over and everyone applauded. Kurt wondered if the applause wasn't more because it had ended than in appreciation for its contents, but the speaker would never know the difference.

Next, the chairman of the school board stepped to the microphone and began, "Will the members of the senior class of Willard High School please rise."

As they stood, there was the usual scraping of metal chairs on the wooden gym floor. The school had an auditorium, but it wasn't nearly large enough to accommodate all of the friends and relatives of the graduates, so chairs had been set up in the gym, and a temporary platform built along one wall.

"By the authority vested in me by the Board of Education, I now certify that the students whose names I will call have fulfilled all of the requirements for graduation from Willard High School. Will the graduates come to the platform as their names are called to receive their diplomas."

All of this had been rehearsed that morning, so with the precision of toy soldiers, the seniors moved out of the rows and began forming a line leading to the platform.

Kurt had spent four years with most of the kids standing in line with him, and he knew them well. He was, however, having difficulty recognizing some of them. He assumed that was Peter just behind him. This was the first time Kurt had ever seen Pete wearing a tie, and from the distressed look on Pete's face, Kurt knew the tie would come off the minute the ceremonies were over.

And there was Ric across the aisle. He hadn't

been to a barber since before Christmas, but there he was, standing in line with a new haircut, looking more like a model all-American boy than the rebel he had tried to be all four years.

Even Tammy, standing directly in front of Kurt, looked different in nylons and heels. Kurt had never seen her in anything but jeans and tennis shoes.

A suit and tie weren't unusual for Kurt, but he felt especially dressed up in his new grey suit and burgundy tie. He hadn't planned on getting a new suit for graduation, but his dad had insisted, and Kurt wasn't about to pass up the opportunity for some new clothes.

The principal's voice over the P.A. system, calling "Alice Adams," jolted Kurt back to reality.

Alice walked up the three steps to the platform, extending her left hand for the diploma, and her right hand to shake the principal's hand—just as it had been rehearsed that morning.

"Poor Alice," Kurt thought. "She's been first in everything for twelve years. With A.A. as initials, she was in the front row of every class, and generally called upon first." Kurt wondered why some creative teacher had never thought of being different and starting the seating assignments with "Z."

Kurt was about midway in the line because his name was Lang. "Kinda symbolic," Kurt thought. "I've been just about the middle of everything all my life."

And it was true. He had never failed a class, but on the other hand he had never received an "A" in anything but one English class in which he had spent most of his time working on the school paper. He had become fascinated with laying out a paper, and had spent many hours that semester in the *Clarion* office. From that time on, he had continued to work on the school paper in one capacity or another, and had become good friends with Mr. Heraldson, the faculty advisor to the *Clarion*.

Every teacher since kindergarten had put on Kurt's record that he wasn't working up to his potential, but long ago he had decided that the middle of the class was a nice comfortable place to be. There he didn't get hassled too much by teachers for poor grades, but neither did they expect him to know all the answers in class discussion. Kurt liked the anonymity being Mr. Average gave him.

And what was true academically was also true morally and ethically. He had never been a bad kid—never got into any serious trouble either at home or school—but he wasn't exactly an angel either. He had been sent to the principal's office a few times in junior high, but

13

by high school had learned the limits of his teachers' tolerance, and had stayed clear of the principal.

The church had been a big influence on Kurt's life. A junior high Sunday School teacher had talked to him about the need for accepting Christ as Savior, and he had done so, then and there. From that time on there had never been a question in Kurt's mind that he was a Christian, but, on the other hand, he had never really been turned on for Christ like some of the other kids.

And just like his place at school, Kurt was satisfied with his middle-of-the-road Christianity. No one really expected him to get too involved in church or youth group activities— that was left up to the more spiritual.

Most people at church considered it a miracle that Kurt was a Christian at all. His mother had died when he was eight, and his father had never re-married, raising him alone with the help of a few housekeepers who had come and gone through the years.

His father was a good middle-class, moral citizen. But, as an accountant in a small law office, he worked long hours. When Sunday came, he preferred to sleep in or go to the golf course.

It was the next-door neighbors, the Johnstons, who began taking Kurt to Sunday School soon after his mother died. And it was the Johnstons who were largely responsible for Kurt's spiritual development. Many people at church thought Kurt was the Johnston's son, and that Cindy, their daughter, was Kurt's sister. They were the same age and in the same grade, but no one seemed to have thought about that.

So, here was Kurt, just where he belonged—in the middle of the line, in a middle-class school, in the middle of his class standings, of average moral and spiritual development, waiting for a diploma that would allow him to go into a middle-class world and try to make a moderate success at life.

From Adams, the line moved through Baxter, Carter, Dover, and then to the Knoxes. By that time, Kurt was standing in front of the platform with only three students ahead of him.

Everything went off as planned with the exception of the occasional, but expected, goof. Some girl, unaccustomed to wearing high heels, stumbled up the steps, and several boys forgot which hand to use when reaching for the diploma.

Then he heard the name, "Kurt Brian Lang," and he stepped up to get his diploma. As he left the stage, diploma in hand, he turned toward the audience and smiled. This was for his father's benefit. He knew his father would be in the aisle with his camera cocked, waiting to immortalize that moment. Parents always seemed more secure with a picture to prove to their friends and relatives that their kid really did graduate.

Kurt moved back to his seat, and when the row was filled, everyone sat down—just as it had been rehearsed. Like everyone else, he immediately opened the black cover to see if there was really anything in it. He had waited twelve years for this moment, and he wouldn't really believe it was all over until he saw the signed diploma with his own eyes.

Graduation day is something a student begins to think about in junior high. At first, it is just a glimmer of hope far beyond the horizon, but by the time he or she enters senior high it becomes a real, bona fide dream.

And then comes the senior year, and everything from the first day of school is geared to that one, final, grand, climactic event—graduation. Days are counted based upon graduation day. Tests are taken with the idea that somehow they contribute to getting that piece of parchment wrapped in imitation black leather. And early in the year, the guys begin to jockey themselves into a position where they will be assured of having a date for the graduation weekend festivities. It was kind of an unwritten rule at Willard High that when you asked someone for a date to the prom, it meant you were also asking them for the graduation night party.

Kurt knew he had gotten into the dating game late, but he was ready for graduation weekend. Terri was his date, and before the night was over, he was determined to have a closer relationship with her—and graduate in more ways than one.

But we're getting ahead of the story. And like the Red King told Alice, a story should begin at the beginning. So this story will begin with the entrance of a real, live female into Kurt's otherwise ho-hum life.

A New Girl in Town

It was the Monday morning following Thanksgiving vacation when he first saw her. After three months of school, everyone knew everyone else on the bus. So when a new girl came out of a house on Fourth Avenue and began walking toward the bus, every head turned in that direction.

Kurt had never seen anything so beautiful, and he would remember that first morning the rest of his life. The way she walked, the way her brown hair reflected the early morning light, the way she smiled when the guys on the bus whistled—he would remember it all.

By the time the bus reached school, Kurt had made an important decision. It was now or never for him. For the first time in his life, he was going to excel at something. His chances of making it with a new girl were as good as anyone else's, and he was determined to move in before the other guys had a chance. This would be the biggest challenge of his life, but the surge of excitement which coursed through his whole body and mind told him he was ready for it.

Chasing a female was going to be a new experience for Kurt. Along with the rest of his "Mr. Average" personality, he had never really excelled with women. It wasn't that he didn't like them, or that they didn't like him. He felt very much at ease in a group of girls. They came to him for help with assignments, for rides to games, or for company at lunch. But when it came time for an honest-to-goodness date, they usually turned to some super-jock, and Kurt had never done anything to stop them.

Kurt was of average weight and height for his age, but the one thing which made him stand out in any crowd was his very fine, platinum blond hair which he tried to part in the middle, but which usually ended up as bangs just above his eyes. A few years earlier he had gone through a period of hating his hair because he thought it looked too much like a girl's. But in recent years he had come to accept it as part of his individuality. He had never heard anyone call him handsome, but he had overheard some girls call him cute. He had a clear complexion and this, together with soft blue eyes and lips that made him look like he was smiling even when he wasn't, were definite assets.

To top off his physical appearance, he was always neatly dressed. It was important to his dad to have his son dressed as well as any of the other kids in school, so he saw to it that there was always money available for clothes which Kurt wanted or needed. Kurt also worked part-time in a men's clothing store where he could pick up on any new style.

So, he was confident of his looks. But he wasn't tall enough, or fast enough to make it big in basketball, and he wasn't muscular enough to withstand a block in football. He had tried baseball one year, but spent most of the time on the bench when he slid into home base and broke his ankle in the first game of the season. Unfortunately, at Willard High, if you couldn't make it big in some sport, you had difficulty making it big with the girls.

So deciding to give a new girl a chase—and doing it—were two different things. His hundred-yard-dash into romance started with a stumble. His first encounter with the new girl came at lunch the first day, and the results were not encouraging. It went something like this:

"Hello."

"Hi."

"You're new, aren't you?"

"Yes."

"Just moved in?"

"Now what do you think? I wouldn't be starting school this late in the year if I hadn't."

"Yeah, guess so," Kurt stammered. "What's your na . . . ."

But by that time she had picked up her tray and was heading off to a table of girls without even looking back to see who had been talking to her.

Even that brief exchange came only after Kurt had pushed and shoved, inviting the wrath of a guy twice his size, just so that he could get into the cafeteria line behind her.

But he remained undaunted—and optimistic. That evening, he spent much of his normal study time developing a plan of attack. He thought of trying to catch her alone by her locker, but he didn't know her locker number. To make matters worse, he still didn't even know her name. He could, of course, try the direct approach again, but the thought of her walking away a second time sent chills up and down his spine. He didn't know if his ego was strong enough to take another put-down like that.

He finally decided to enlist Cindy's help. She had the uncanny knack of finding out everything about any new girl who showed up at school. Within twenty-four hours after their arrival she would know who they were, where they had come from, why they had moved, and if she was going to like them. Yes, he would ask Cindy. After all, she owed him a favor. He had introduced Brad to her, and now they were dating regularly.

Cindy Johnston was the girl next door. It was her folks who had taken Kurt to church and Sunday School, so he had grown up with Cindy and thought of her as a sister. They had played in the same sand box, shared the same toys, and after Kurt's mother died, he had spent many hours at the Johnstons' house.

Cindy was a good friend—and only that. He never thought of her in any other way. Occasionally someone would tease him about Cindy, but he would just shrug it off and say, "Aw, we're too good of friends to spoil it by dating."

It seemed more difficult to be romantic with someone you remembered riding your tricycle and wiping her nose on her coat sleeve. Also Cindy took her Christianity much too seriously to please Kurt. It seemed she was always going to church for something. After Kurt had started to drive to church by himself, he had learned to say "no" to some of Cindy's invitations to church activities.

But Cindy didn't seem to mind. She seemed content just to remain a good friend, and Kurt knew he could trust her with any secret. They had shared many things through the years.

So, as they were walking home from the bus the next night, Kurt said, "Cindy, you've got to help me."

"Anything but history," she answered with a teasing smile. "You know how I hate it."

"It's much more important than that," Kurt said.

"You're about to flunk history, and there's something more important than that?"

"It's a girl," Kurt admitted weakly.

"Kurt!" Cindy stopped walking and turned toward him. "Did I hear you right? A girl?"

"Sure, what's so odd about that?"

"It's just . . . just that you've never seemed interested in a girl before. I didn't know you knew the difference."

"Aw, get off my back. Remember, I've lived next door to a girl for seventeen years, and she's taught me a few things."

"I always thought you considered me the guy next door."

"Come on, forget the insults. Are you going to help me, or aren't you?"

"I usually do, although I don't know why."

"Well, there's this new girl that's been riding our bus this week. I'm sure you've noticed her. But she gets on after we do, and gets off at night before we do, so I never get a chance to talk to her. The bus is always so crowded by the time she gets on, I don't even get near her."

"Then why don't you just walk up to her in the hall and ask her who she is?"

"You know me better than that," Kurt said, almost pleading.

"Yes, I guess I do. You *do* have a problem. Are you talking about that brunette with the little southern accent who started school Monday?"

"That's the one," Kurt said, his eyes getting wider. "Please find out what you can about her."

"Kurt Lang, I've never seen you so excited about anything in my life. That southern charm must have really made an impression to turn you on like that. She may seem different after you get to know her better."

"I'll take my chances. Let me decide for myself. Okay?"

"Okay, but don't say I didn't warn you. If you want to know her name, that's easy, I've already met her."

"I knew I could depend upon you. What is it?"

"It's Terri Turner, and she's from Dallas, Texas." Then Cindy laughed. "Terri Turner from Texas. That almost rhymes."

"Know anything else?"

"Give me time," Cindy answered. "She's only been here three days."

"See what else you can find out," Kurt

pleaded. "You know, 'Is she going steady,' et cetera."

"I'm not playing matchmaker for you or anyone else," Cindy said. "I have enough trouble with my own love life."

"See what you can do," Kurt said. "This sort of investigation is your specialty."

"I'm not sure if that's a compliment or an insult." Cindy replied. "But I'll see what I can do."

With that Kurt and Cindy parted and each went up their separate sidewalks.

The next night as they were walking home again, Cindy said, "I don't know why I should knock myself out for you, but I do have some information."

"Far out!" Kurt exclaimed, breaking his stride and pulling Cindy around so she would face him. "What is it?"

"You *are* anxious, aren't you?" she teased.

"Come on, Cindy, quit stalling," Kurt begged.

"Well, there are a lot of rumors floating around school, and it's hard to separate fact from rumor. I did find out that she is living with her aunt, Jan Holmgren. You know her, she goes to our church, but she keeps pretty much to herself. People don't know much about her. She seems to have plenty of money, but she doesn't work, and no one seems to know how she made it.

"And no one knows for sure why Terri changed schools in the middle of her senior year. Some think she got kicked out of school in Texas. But somebody told me her mother and father got a divorce, so she came to live with her aunt. I'm going with that story 'cause she seems much too nice to have been kicked out of school. But one never knows. There's something different about that girl, and I can't quite decide what it is."

"That's my Cindy," Kurt said, giving her a little hug. "Not only does she know her name, but her relatives' names and all of the rumors floating around about her. Thanks a million! You won't tell anyone that I asked you, will you?"

"I'd love to, but you know too much about me. It wouldn't be safe," Cindy answered with a chuckle.

"I knew I could trust you," Kurt said.

"Just don't blame me if there is a snake under that beautiful skin," Cindy said.

"Don't worry," Kurt answered. "I was a Boy Scout, and learned all about how to handle snakes."

"Well, get out the manual and review it. You may need it."

Kurt Makes His Move

Armed with her name, Kurt was now ready to make his first move. He got Terri's locker number from a friend who worked in the principal's office, and began walking by her locker between classes. This tactic resulted in a couple of eye contacts, and one "Hi," but that was all.

His next move came in the cafeteria. Kurt and his friend, Brad, were walking around with their trays looking for a place to sit when Kurt noticed two places across from Terri and another girl. Kurt motioned for Brad to follow him.

The girls were talking, so they didn't notice the guys sit down. Kurt was taking a big bite of a ham sandwich, and Terri had just opened her mouth for another spoonful of soup when their eyes met across the table. Kurt stopped chewing, and Terri's spoon remained suspended in space for a moment. After what seemed like an eternity to Kurt, Terri smiled, and he returned the smile—as best he could with a mouth full of ham sandwich.

Then they both went back to eating. Terri continued to visit with the girl beside her, and Kurt made idle talk with Brad. The girls finished first, and as they picked up their trays to leave, Terri looked back at Kurt and said, "See you around."

Kurt was ecstatic. For the first time he was sure she had really noticed him . . . now things would be easier. When they were gone, Brad looked at Kurt and said, "Come on back to earth, man. You look like you're ready to go into orbit. If you're so hot on her, why don't you do something about it?"

"I am. Give me time. I'm new at this, you know. She spoke to me—that's progress."

"It will take more than 'See you around,' if you plan to make any headway with her. There are a lot of other guys around school who have noticed her, too."

"They better not horn in on my territory. I've staked claim to her, and I intend to protect my claim."

"You'd better let her in on this territorial claim soon, or she might not even know how lucky she is," Brad said, laughing.

30

"Go ahead and laugh." Kurt retorted, as they started down the hall. "By graduation night, she'll be mine. Just you wait and see."

"You are serious, aren't you?" Brad said, his face losing its smile.

"I've never been more serious in my life," Kurt answered.

"I don't know what's come over you. This isn't the Kurt I know," Brad said, shaking his head, "but good luck."

And with that they went their separate ways to class.

Kurt's second break came the next morning before school started. He was returning a book he'd taken out on overnight reserve to the library when he noticed Cindy waving for him to come over to a table. That wasn't unusual. Cindy often did that. But when Kurt neared the table, he saw that she wasn't alone. Seated across from her was Terri.

"Not a matchmaker," Kurt chuckled to himself. "I wonder what she calls this?"

"Hi, Kurt," Cindy said. "We were just talking about you."

"How depressing," Kurt said, dropping in the chair by Cindy.

"Not at all. I was just telling Terri here ... you know Terri, don't you?"

"Well, I've seen her around, but we haven't formally met," Kurt answered.

"Terri, this is my neighbor, Kurt. Kurt, this is the girl who just moved into the house up on Fourth Avenue and has been riding our bus this week."

"Hi, Kurt," Terri said, in a voice that was as smooth and soft as if dipped in honey.

"Glad to meet you," Kurt answered, almost choking on his words. A quick glance in Cindy's direction showed she was trying desperately not to laugh.

"So, what garbage were you feeding Terri about me?" Kurt asked. "You really shouldn't color her thinking until she has had an opportunity to find out for herself."

"No garbage, just food for thought," Cindy answered. "I told her that we've been friends since kindergarten."

"Actually, before that," Kurt said. "Our parents let us take our naps in the same crib."

"How cozy," Terri said, almost purring.

"Of course, I wasn't old enough to protect myself from her aggressive behavior," Kurt said.

"Nor did you want to," Cindy answered.

"Now you're bragging."

"Was he always this cute?" Terri asked Cindy. Kurt couldn't tell if she was being serious or sarcastic.

"Oh, you should have seen him in diapers," Cindy answered.

"Hey, you can't remember that," Kurt said, blushing a little. "You were in diapers at the same time, you know. After all, you're only two months older than me."

"Three months," Cindy corrected him. "My birthday is in May, and yours is in July. I always remembered that because your mother would take all of the neighborhood kids to the beach on your birthday."

For lack of a comeback, and to get Cindy off his back, Kurt looked at Terri and asked, "And when's your birthday?"

"In January, I think," Terri answered, her eyes becoming serious.

"You think?" Cindy and Kurt said almost in unison.

"My mother always told me it was in March, and that's when I celebrated it, but I finally got a birth certificate last year so that I could get a Social Security number, and it gave my birthdate as January 17. When I asked about it, my mother sorta shrugged her shoulders and said, 'There must have been some mistake.' "

"Sounds as if she was trying to hide something," Kurt said.

"She's probably got a lot to hide," Terri answered, looking down at the book before her. "Her life has been pretty well mixed up."

There was an awkward silence, and then Kurt said, "I'm sorry."

"Oh, don't be," Terri said, smiling again. "Things are going to be okay now."

"Now that you are living with your aunt?" Cindy asked.

"Yes. Now that I'm with Jan . . . but that's another story," Terri said just as the bell rang.

As they left the library, Kurt asked, "To be continued?"

"What? My life story?" Terri asked.

"No, I just meant . . . well, you know what I mean," Kurt stammered.

"If you like," Terri answered. "I need some friends like you two. It's kinda lonely starting a new school and . . . and a new life."

That conversation broke the ice, and Kurt started to spend a lot of time with Terri around school. Other guys were making obvious moves to get her attention, but whenever she saw Kurt, she would leave the others and join him.

But he still had little time with her alone. Lunch together usually meant a foursome— Kurt, Cindy, Brad, and Terri. They talked about many things, but Terri would often look off into space as if she were dreaming. Now that he had had an opportunity to study her face, he thought he could see a maturity beyond her years. She would laugh at some remark by one of the other three, but then suddenly, her eyes would become serious again, and Kurt would wonder if she were about to cry. He longed to know her better. Even with the sadness in her face and eyes, she was the most beautiful girl he had ever seen, but somehow, she seemed so different—so aloof and almost cold.

Kurt and Cindy talked about it several times.

"I like her, but I just can't get to know her," Cindy said one night on their way home from the bus.

"I know what you mean," Kurt answered. "She seems as if she's in another world—it's almost spooky at times."

"There's a lot more than either of us know—a lot she isn't telling us," Cindy said. "I still wonder why she really came to live with Jan."

"I hope to find out some day," Kurt answered.

"I just hope you won't be sorry when you do," Cindy said.

"What do you mean by that remark?" Kurt said indignantly.

"I'm not sure exactly. But you may find out more than you want to know. Maybe your angel really isn't so angelic," she answered.

"Let's give her the benefit of the doubt," Kurt said.

"I intend to," Cindy answered, "but as I said earlier, don't blame me if you get burned."

One night after school the following week, Kurt got off the bus when Terri did.

"Mind if I tag along? " Kurt asked, coming up beside her on the sidewalk.

"If you're willing to walk eight blocks home just to go one block with me, I guess I shouldn't mind—I should be flattered," Terri said.

It had been an especially warm fall, but now, with the coming of December, the weather had suddenly changed. A cold, biting wind was coming out of the northwest, blowing the fallen leaves across the sidewalk in front of Kurt and Terri. Walking along beside her, Kurt realized for the first time how short she really was. He was only 5 feet 9 inches, and yet he could look down on her long brown hair which was being whipped around in the wind, occasionally covering her eyes. She had to keep pushing it back with one hand to see where she was going.

They walked along in silence as Kurt tried to think of some way to begin the conversation, but while he was still thinking, she said, "We never finished our discussion the other morning."

"What discussion?" Kurt asked, pretending not to know what she was talking about.

"You wanted to know more about my past, didn't you?"

"I'm not sure I came right out and asked," Kurt said, "but I have to admit I'm curious."

"When I came, I vowed to leave Dallas behind, and not discuss that life with anyone. In fact, I vowed not to make any friends here. I had been hurt too badly in the past. But you and Cindy seem so different . . . so genuinely interested in me."

"I'm glad you feel that way. We . . . at least I . . . really do want to get to know you," Kurt said, moving closer so that their shoulders were touching as they walked.

"I'm not sure that's possible," Terri said. "I don't really know myself, so I can't expect someone else to know me."

"Let's just say I want to try," Kurt answered. "I'm not really concerned about your past. I'm just glad it led you here."

"Thanks, Kurt. I needed that, but if you knew the whole story you might not say that."

"Try me."

"My life has been so different from yours that it would be hard for you to understand. You and Cindy both come from loving homes, but my father and mother never did get along too well. Both of them drank heavily, and dad was frequently out of work. I always seemed like an extra burden to them. Whenever things got too bad, Jan would come to my rescue."

"Your aunt?"

"Yes, Aunt Jan. I understand you know her."

"No one really knows her either," Kurt said. "She reminds me a lot of you. She seems so mysterious, almost aloof."

"That's Jan. She's quiet until you get to know

her. But she has a heart of gold, and is really very sweet and generous. She always sent me money when I really needed it. This summer and fall things kept going from bad to worse in my life, and Jan asked if I wanted to come up here and live with her. I guess she figured she might just as well support me here as back in Texas."

"Sounds like she's wealthy," Kurt said.

"Not wealthy by some people's standards, but she lives comfortably, and is certainly wealthy compared to my parents. They were always jealous of her money, and thought she could give them more."

By this time they were standing by the end of the sidewalk leading up to the two-story colonial house where Jan and Terri lived.

"Want to come in for a little while?" Terri asked. "It's cold out here."

"Just for a few minutes," Kurt said. "I have to work tonight."

Terri got out her key, opened the front door, and the two of them stepped into the front hall. It was a wide hallway with a stairway leading up to the second floor. On the one side, Kurt could see a formal dining room, big enough to accommodate a large family, and on the other side of the hall was the living room.

"Far out!" Kurt exclaimed. "Dad and I don't have anything like this."

"You and your dad? What about your mother?" Terri asked as she led him into the living room.

"I thought Cindy would have told you—she seems to have told everything else."

"You see? I don't know you very well either," Terri said.

"My mother died when I was eight, and dad and I have lived alone ever since."

"I'm sorry," Terri said, pulling off her jacket and sitting down on the quilted sofa.

Kurt took off his jacket, and sat down beside her.

"Oh, don't be sorry," he said. "I've had a good life. Sometimes I used to envy other kids whose mothers came to school to pick them up, and have parties for them. But dad and I have always gotten along well. He doesn't hassle me, and has always bought just about every-thing I needed or wanted. He's been a good dad. I guess no mother is better than a bad one."

"Right now, I envy you," Terri said, her green eyes again becoming serious.

"You were talking about Jan," Kurt said.

"As I said, Jan isn't exactly wealthy, but as you can see, she lives comfortably. I'm not even sure where she got her money. She has never worked as long as I can remember. At home there was a rumor that a rich man died and left this house and some money to her, but she never talks about it. She's always been good to me. Just about everything I have—my clothes, my watch, my stereo—all came from her." Her voice trailed off as if she were in deep thought.

Both were silent, and then Terri said, as she stood up, "Yes, I owe a lot to Jan."

Kurt stood up, too, and picked up his coat. "Better get going," he said.

As he started toward the door, Terri said "Are you going to be home later tonight?"

"I guess so, why?" Kurt asked. He wasn't sure what his dad had planned, but if she wanted him to be home, everything else was automatically cancelled.

"I have to ask you something," Terri said. "I'll call."

"Can't you ask me now?"

"No, I'll call," Terri insisted.

"I get off work at 8:00," Kurt said as he closed the door.

TERRI'S MOVE

Kurt made record time getting home that night, but found it difficult to concentrate on his English assignment. Instead of studying in his room as he usually did, he brought his books down to the living room and sat in a big chair near the phone. Twice the phone rang, but each time it was for his dad. He tried not to seem overly anxious but it was difficult. When his dad was thirty-four minutes (he timed it) talking to a client, Kurt had visions of Terri trying to call, and then finally giving up.

But about 9:30, the phone rang again, and when Kurt answered, there was that unmistakable, smooth, honey-coated voice on the other end.

"Kurt?"

"Yeah."

"Busy?"

"Naw, just trying to read Macbeth. How about you?"

"I'm studying for a biology test tomorrow, but I don't know a butterfly from a grasshopper."

"Aw, biology is easy. I took it last year and aced it. Well, not quite. I got a B but I never studied."

"Maybe you could teach me?" Terri said.

"Is that a date?" Kurt teased.

"No, but that's what I called about."

"Biology?"

"No, about a date."

Kurt had dreamed of asking Terri for a date, but here she was doing the asking. The incongruity of it made him laugh.

"Are you laughing at me?" Terri said, obviously annoyed.

"No, you know better. I was just thinking how much I wanted to ask you that." He had blurted it out before he realized what he was saying.

"Really? Here I've been trying to decide all evening if I should call. I thought maybe Cindy had already asked you to go to the Sadie Hawkins party next week."

"Cindy? She would never do anything like that. In fact, no girl has ever done that. There's nothing between Cindy and me. We're just good friends. Cindy is more like a sister to me," Kurt said.

"I've never heard a sister talk that much about her brother," Terri answered.

"Aw, you're dreaming," Kurt said. "She doesn't care if I live or die. Anyway, Cindy only goes with real spiritual guys. I'm not sure I'm good enough for her. Besides, she's already asked Brad."

"Wow, you *are* blind," Terri exclaimed. "I can see why Cindy said you have been getting failing grades in your social life. But you haven't answered my question."

"You haven't asked me anything yet."

"Don't be so difficult," Terri said, exasperated. "You know what I'm talking about. Will you go with me to the Sadie Hawkins party?"

"Sure, that would be fun," Kurt answered.

"Great," Terri answered, sounding relieved. "We never had Sadie Hawkins parties in Dallas, so I haven't had much practice in asking guys for dates."

They spent the next 45 minutes talking about school, other kids and music. During the conversation, Kurt began to realize just how different their worlds had been. She had never heard of many of his favorite recording artists, and he had only read about some she considered top groups or singers. But when he hung up, he was satisfied with the conversation.

He felt he was making progress, not only with her, but with girls in general.

He couldn't study after that—not that he had done much before the call. So he went upstairs, got undressed and lay on his bed with his eyes wide open for a long time. He had always dreamed of falling in love, but never thought it would be the middle of his senior year before he did. Other guys were falling madly in and out of love by the time they were freshmen, but not Kurt. Some of the guys were beginning to make remarks to him about it. Even Brad said once, when he was flying two feet off the ground over some girl, "What's the matter, Kurt? Is there something wrong with you? Any normal guy falls in love."

"Just waiting for the right one," Kurt had answered. But deep inside he was beginning to wonder if he would ever really fall in love. He had lots of friends who were girls, but no girlfriends. Maybe he was failing in his social life, as Cindy said, but somehow he resented her saying it. Without a mother there had never been much social life around his house. His opportunity for social interaction with people had been limited. Maybe he had never really learned how to appreciate and love another person.

These were the thoughts going through his mind that night. But as he analyzed his feelings, he realized he had found someone, finally, that he cared for very much. And maybe this was love. Time would tell.

The Sadie Hawkins party was the topic of conversation at lunch the next day.

"I'll never understand why we need Sadie Hawkins day," Brad exclaimed. "What happened to the good ol' days when a guy asked the girl for a date?"

"Listen to grandpa," Cindy said. "It's about time girls have an opportunity to take the initiative. Now maybe the guys will know what it's like to sit at home and wait for someone to call."

"I wasn't sitting at home waiting for your call," Brad snapped back. "You tripped me in the hall the day after the party was announced."

"You're wrong. It was the same day," Cindy snickered.

"Well, it's not fair to ask a girl to go through all of the agony of making a call for a date. It's different with guys. It's second nature to them."

"Listen to the pro," Kurt laughed.

"I forgot you haven't had as much practice as some of us," Brad teased.

"He probably wasn't sitting at home waiting for my call either," Terri said.

Kurt didn't answer.

"Well, Kurt . . . " Brad said. "Were you waiting for her call?"

Kurt blushed.

"You mean, you were?" Terri asked. "If I had known that I would have called earlier."

"If you had, both of us would have gotten a lot more studying done," Kurt admitted.

"Well, now that we're all honest with one another, we can discuss what we're going to do after the party," Brad said.

"I thought you knew," Cindy answered.

"Knew what?"

"A bunch of kids from church are getting together after the party. I've already told them you were coming," Cindy said.

"We're not going to church," Terri said quickly, and then, looking at Kurt, added, "are we?"

"Whatever you say," Kurt answered. "You asked me on this date. Remember?"

"Jan reminded me of the party at church, but I didn't promise her I would go," Terri said. "I've heard about a number of parties we could go to. Fact is, Jim Hagen has invited us over to his house. His folks are in Florida, so he has the house to himself."

"And what a house!" Brad exclaimed.

"Yeah, his dad is just about the richest guy in Twin Falls, and his house looks like it," Kurt added.

"I've heard about the kind of parties Jim puts on," Cindy said.

"We can handle it," Kurt answered.

46

"Maybe you need a chaperon," Brad said.

"Brad Larson, you're going with me," Cindy declared.

"You heard her," Kurt replied. "You're going with her."

"What a man won't do for a woman," Brad said, shaking his head.

As Kurt and Cindy were walking home from the bus that night, Cindy brought up the subject of the party again. "Do you really think you should go to Jim's party?" she asked.

"Sure, why not?"

"You've heard about his parties, haven't you?"

"I've heard they're lots of fun," Kurt answered.

"If liquor and drugs are what you call fun," Cindy answered.

"You've never been there, so how would you know?" Kurt answered. "Besides, you don't have to indulge just because you're there."

"Maybe not, but I just don't think it's any place for a Christian," Cindy said. "And what kind of a testimony is it to Terri?"

"I suppose you think everyone should be in church like you," Kurt said. "Let's not scare Terri off. There will be plenty of time to talk to her about spiritual things."

"I didn't say everyone should be in church, but it just seems like common sense to stay out of trouble when you know it's there."

47

"But you don't know. You've just heard," Kurt insisted.

"Maybe. But I've heard enough to stay away."

"Thanks for the advice, but this time I'm not following it," Kurt said. "All my life I've gone to you for advice and help, but this is my first really important date, and you're not going to blow it for me."

"It's your life," Cindy shot back as she turned up her sidewalk.

THE PARTY—AND AFTER

The night of the Sadie Hawkins party Terri picked Kurt up in her aunt's Buick as she had promised. She didn't offer to let him drive, so he slipped into the passenger's side and she drove to school. The switching of roles seemed awkward to him, and he wasn't sure he liked it. This wasn't quite the way he had envisioned a first date with Terri, but they were together, and that's what really counted.

The party was well planned with something for everyone. An arcade had been set up in one room with various electronic games, a full-length movie was going on in another, and booths were set up around the edge of the gym, sponsored by various organizations. Some of the booths offered food, and others games of chance and skill.

Kurt and Terri spent most of the evening with Brad and Cindy. They watched the movie for a little while, but both Brad and Terri had seen it before, so they all decided to leave. They ended up spending much of the evening drinking pop, eating hotdogs, and just talking. Kurt did win a doll at a ring toss booth, and promptly presented it to Terri.

At 10:00 p.m. a band set up on one end of the gym and began to play. As the music started, Kurt looked around and asked, "Where are Cindy and Brad?"

"Oh, they left already," Terri answered. "Cindy doesn't dance, you know, and besides, she's the chairperson of the committee for the church party. She wanted to get there before the others."

"I'll bet Brad went away kicking and screaming," Kurt said, laughing at the thought.

"Actually, he was blindfolded, gagged, and handcuffed," Terri replied.

They stood on the side for a little while watching the others before Terri said, "Come on, let's dance."

"I warn you, I don't know much about dancing," Kurt said.

"That's okay, I'll teach you," Terri said, taking

him by the arm and leading him onto the floor.

"Right now, I'm extremely teachable," Kurt replied, as he felt her warm hand on his arm.

As they went from one number to another, Kurt began to catch on and loosen up. Finally, he pulled Terri over to some empty chairs where they both collapsed, laughing and breathless.

"You'll have to admit that wasn't bad for the first time. I didn't even step on your feet," Kurt said.

"Why haven't you danced before?" Terri asked. "Are you like Cindy?"

"No, not really. Although I'm sure she has had some influence on me. It's just that I've never dated much, and it's rather difficult to dance with yourself. Besides, most of my social life has been with the kids at some church function . . . and they don't dance there."

"Why haven't you dated much?" Terri asked, pressing the issue.

"I can't really answer that. It's just that I was an only child, as I told you, and after my mother died, our house was pretty quiet. I just became a loner. That's why I've enjoyed working on the school paper instead of going out for sports. That's something I can do by myself. I guess I grew up thinking girls wouldn't want to go with me. I wasn't Joe Cool, or a super-jock. I was just

Mr. Average, and the girls around here don't seem to have much time for average guys."

"Hey, don't put yourself down like that. You've got everything it takes. You're quite attractive, and that hair! Most girls would love to have it."

"Yeah, on a girl, but not on a guy," Kurt said.

"But it's you. It's what makes you special," Terri said. "Lots of the girls like you. I've heard them talk about you."

"Why haven't they ever told me?" Kurt said.

"Maybe you've never given them a chance. By the way, you didn't seem timid when you started to chase me."

"You noticed?"

"How could I help but notice! Why me?"

"Because I've never met or seen a girl like you before. That's why," Kurt answered honestly.

Terri didn't respond, but moved her body closer to Kurt and he reached out his arm and put it around her.

Around 11:30 p.m., some of the kids began to leave, and Kurt noticed that Jim Hagen and several of his friends had left.

"When do you have to be in?" Terri asked.

"I told my dad I should be home by 1:00 a.m., but he doesn't wait up for me, and he won't get too upset if it's later."

"I told Jan I would have her car home by 1:00

a.m., and since this is the first time she's let me use it, I think I'd better get it back on time, or she'll never let me use it again."

"Are you afraid of her?" Kurt asked.

"No, it's just that right now I don't have a choice. I have to do what she says."

"I don't understand," Kurt said.

"I can't explain now, but I will sometime," Terri said, and then quickly changed the subject. "Ready to go to Jim's house?"

"Sure, why not?" Kurt answered. He didn't pursue her remark, but he wondered what she meant by it. He was beginning to realize just how much there was about Terri that he didn't know . . . and he wasn't sure how much he wanted to know. Maybe it was better this way.

Kurt had been to the Hagens' house once when he'd gone out for baseball. Jim had invited the whole team over for an evening. So Terri gave Kurt the keys to Jan's car and said, "Since you know the way, you drive."

Jim's house was set on a hill overlooking the city. It was long and rambling, but didn't look as large as it really was when viewed from the drive. The back side, facing the edge of the cliff, had a two story walk-out with a large family room on the ground level, and just outside, under a heated plastic bubble, a swimming pool.

53

Terri and Kurt drove partway up the circular drive, and parked. There were already about a dozen cars there, so they had to walk a little way to the house. The door was standing slightly open, so they walked in without ringing the bell. Directly in front of them was the living room, and since they could see a number of kids in there, they headed in that direction.

"I can see what you mean by this house," Terri said. "I'm not used to such luxury. It's much nicer than Jan's."

When they entered the living room, Jim was standing in the middle of the floor, holding a beer, and surrounded by a group of friends. When he saw Terri and Kurt, he left the circle and came over to them.

"Welcome to my pad," he said to Terri. "Kurt's been here before."

"It's more a mansion than a pad," Terri said, looking around in amazement.

"Not bad for parties . . . especially when the folks are out of town," Jim said with a wink.

"Don't they hire spies?" Terri asked.

"Naw, they trust me," Jim answered. "Of course, if they only knew . . . " But he never finished the sentence.

"I guess you can't tell parents everything," Kurt said. "It isn't healthy for them."

"Well, Terri," Jim said. "If you get tired of the freshman here, just dump him and let a graduate show you around."

"Hey, lay off," Kurt said. "She's mine . . . at least for tonight."

"Sorry, ol' man. I was just trying to be a good host. The house is yours, do anything you like. Some of the kids are downstairs playing pool, and others are getting ready for a swim. There's beer and soft drinks in the refrigerator in the family room. Help yourself."

"He's something else," Terri said, as they began to walk down the steps to the lower level.

"He's a big bag of wind," Kurt shot back.

"What do you have against him?"

"It's just that he's been the best in everything he's ever tried. He never fails at anything. He always makes the rest of us look bad, and to top it off, he never lets anyone forget it."

"You're just jealous," Terri said.

"Maybe so, but I still don't like him."

"Well, at least you can be civil to him while we're his guests," Terri said.

They stood around the pool table for a little while, and then Kurt asked, "Want something to drink?"

"Sure," Terri answered, so they went over to the refrigerator and Kurt selected a can of pop. Terri took a beer. They arranged a couple of bean bag chairs in front of the fireplace, and settled back to enjoy the fire and their drinks.

"You know, I never dreamed life could be like this," Terri said, staring into the fire.

"What did you expect?"

"It's just that I've never known many fine things in life. Jan's house is the nicest house I've ever lived in. If it wasn't for her, I wouldn't even have decent clothes to wear. Now I have a nice home, good clothes, and . . . you."

"You've probably had a lot of guys chasing after you," Kurt said.

"A few. But some of them really didn't want me, they just wanted my body. And some that I thought loved me, I discovered later were really just using me for their own ends. You're different. Why?"

Kurt didn't answer for a few minutes.

"I'm glad you said different, not odd," Kurt finally said. "I've always considered myself something of a social misfit. You heard Cindy say that I had flunked social."

"I've been a misfit, too, but that was because of my home and my poverty. You don't have that excuse."

"Money may be important, but one needs other things in life. There have been times when I would have traded just about everything I had for one good hug from a mother," Kurt said.

"Maybe we both need the same thing but for different reasons," Terri said.

Once again they remained silent, both staring

into the fire, and completely oblivious to the conversations going on around them.

"Now take Cindy," Terri finally said. "There's someone who is really different . . . in a nice way."

"Like how?" Kurt asked.

"Well, she just seems to have everything put together. I doubt if she ever sits around talking about being a misfit like we're doing. But I do wonder just what she does for fun. It seems all she ever does is go to church."

"Maybe she considers that fun," Kurt said. "Maybe fun is something relative."

"Are you having fun?" Terri asked.

"I really don't know," Kurt said honestly. "I'm enjoying myself, but sometimes I wonder if there isn't more to life than what I've found so far."

Once again they were quiet.

While they were sitting there, Jim entered the room with a middle-aged man. Terri saw him out of the corner of her eye, and sat up in her chair.

"Who's that?" she asked, looking startled.

"Who's who?" Kurt asked.

"That man," Terri said, pointing.

"Oh, he's always around here," Kurt said. "Jim calls him Chester. He was here the last time I was here for a party, and I've seen him around school a few times. I never did find out what connection he has with Jim."

"Kurt, we've got to get out of here," Terri said, getting to her feet.

"Are you crazy? We just got here," Kurt said, trying to pull her back down.

"I'm serious. We've got to get out of here."

"Okay, if you say so, but I can't imagine what's come over you."

"I'll explain later . . . maybe. But right now, come on," she said, pulling him to his feet.

By this time, there were enough people milling around the house that no one noticed Terri and Kurt leave. Kurt helped her into the car, and got into the driver's seat. They were quiet for a few blocks, and then Kurt asked "Want me to take you home? I can walk from your place."

"Would you, please? You won't mind, will you?" Terri sounded as if she were about to cry.

"Naw, the walk will do me good," Kurt said, still puzzled by the turn of events.

They drove to Jan's home in silence, and Kurt helped Terri put the car into the garage. As he turned to go, Terri pulled him back. "I'm sorry," she said. "Really, I am."

Kurt reached out and took her hands. They were cold and trembling.

"I wish you would explain. Is it something . . ."

"No, it's nothing you did. I promise to explain

. . . later. You've been wonderful." Now she started to cry.

Kurt reached out and drew her trembling body to himself. "Thanks for tonight," he whispered into her ear. "I really wish you could tell me what's the matter. Maybe I could help you."

"No. No one can help. You just don't know . . . you can't know," and with that she began to sob again.

Kurt held her tightly and could feel her tears against his cheek. Eventually she quit crying, and he released his hold on her.

"I'll be all right now," Terri said. "See you Monday." And with that she turned and ran toward the house.

Kurt watched until she had gone into the house and had closed the door behind her, then he began to walk slowly home. It was a crisp, cold night. There was no snow on the ground, but all the leaves had fallen, and the full moon shining through the bare branches cast weird shadows on the sidewalk before him.

He tried to think back over the events of the night, and to figure out what might have happened. One minute he was enjoying the company of a beautiful, intelligent, even mature woman, and the next minute he was saying good night to a frightened little girl. He had never experienced anything like it. What could have made her change that fast?

He thought about it long after he went to bed. All of the pieces seemed to fit together except for Chester. It was when Chester had entered the room that Terri went to pieces. But why? What was there about him that could have frightened her? The questions kept coming until the wee hours of the morning, but no answers came with them.

SPECIAL ASSIGNMENT

Kurt went to church on Sunday morning, and then met his dad at the Country Club for dinner. After that he went to Brad's house and watched a football game on TV until time to go to the evening service. After church he went with some of the kids for pizza. It was almost 11:00 p.m. before he got home that night, and he went directly to bed without looking at the Sunday paper.

Kurt had hoped to see Terri at church—especially after the way he'd left her on Friday night—but neither she nor Jan came to either service. So it was Monday morning before he saw her again.

When she got on the bus that morning, Terri looked pale and her eyes were red as if she had been crying. Kurt tried to save a seat for her, but the bus was crowded by the time she got on, and someone took the seat he had saved.

When they arrived at school, Terri got off the bus quickly and went into the school without waiting for Kurt. He tried to follow her, but the five minute warning bell was ringing as he entered the building, so he had to go directly to his first class.

Kurt had third hour free and usually spent it in the *Clarion* office. This morning he went in and checked the assignment board. The *Clarion* came out each Friday, and normally Nancy, the editor, made the assignments for the feature stories on Monday morning. Under his name, he found a note which read, "Do story on drug raid."

"Drug raid? What drug raid?" he said out loud as he read the note.

"You must not have read yesterday's paper," a voice said from across the room.

"Oh, hi, Steve. I didn't see you there. What's this business about a drug raid?"

"Here, read it for yourself," Steve, one of the reporters, said as he tossed a section of the Sunday paper to Kurt.

There on the metro page, in half-inch bold letters, were the words, "POLICE RAID WILLARD HIGH PARTY."

Kurt sat down and began to read aloud, "Police paid a surprise visit to a party being held Friday night at the home of a prominent businessman, Philmore Hagen, at 1615 Summit Avenue."

"Hagen's!" Kurt exclaimed. "I was there, and I didn't see any raid."

"Either you were in hiding, or it happened after you left," Steve said.

Then Kurt remembered their sudden retreat, and said, "I guess we did leave rather early."

The report went on to say that several of the kids had been taken to police headquarters for questioning, and that the investigation was continuing.

"I just can't believe it," Kurt said, putting down the paper. "It seemed like a perfectly normal party to me. I didn't see any evidence of drugs."

"Maybe you don't know what to look for," Nancy said, coming out of a small inner office.

"That's possible," Kurt answered. "I haven't had too much experience with drugs."

"I think everyone, including the principal, is a little surprised by this. Everyone assumes it can't happen at Willard or in Twin Falls. They think drugs are only a problem in New York or Chicago. Maybe none of us realize the extent of the problem. That's why we need a story. You'll need to do some interviewing. Get as many facts as you can, and let's see if we can't wake up the school and our community to the problem."

Steve walked slowly across the room and sat down crosslegged on a desk facing Kurt and Nancy. "Maybe I should be the one doing the story," he said.

"Why?" Nancy asked.

"Because I was pretty heavy into drugs back in the ninth grade, and I've had some experience with it."

"We didn't know," Kurt said.

"Well, I don't exactly have FORMER DRUGGIE printed on my calling card," Steve said.

"Do you really want to do this story?" Nancy asked.

Steve thought for a few moments and then said, "No. I guess I had better stay out of it. I suspect some of my former friends might be involved, and they would think I was out for revenge. If Kurt does it, he's starting from zero. Anything I might say or do would be colored. Kurt doesn't have any enemies—at least not yet."

"And what is that supposed to mean?" Kurt asked.

"The drug business is ruthless. If you start to expose anyone—especially pushers—you had better be prepared to defend yourself."

"How can I make enemies by just reporting the facts as I find them?"

"Sometimes people don't want to hear the facts," Steve answered. "Sometimes people, even parents, like to live in a fantasy world where everything is bright and pure and clean. They can't believe their kids could ever be involved in drugs."

"I'm not sure I want to do this story after listening to you," Kurt said.

"I didn't mean to scare you off," Steve said. "Someone has to do it. All I said was, 'be careful.' This could make or break you as a reporter."

"Since you seem to be our best authority on the subject, give me a hint. Where do I start?" Kurt asked.

"Start by asking questions. Ask the principal, some of the teachers, the students, the police. It won't be long before you get a story. Don't go off on a preaching binge or try to moralize . . . just tell the facts as you find them, and let them speak for themselves."

"Thanks, Steve," Kurt said. "I really appreciate your help. This is beginning to be a bigger job than I anticipated."

"How about getting started," Nancy said, shoving a pencil and notebook into Kurt's hands. "See if you can get a story for next Friday's paper. We have to say something about the raid . . . our readers will expect it."

As Kurt left the *Clarion* office and started

toward the principal's office, he kept thinking about Friday night. He was thankful they had left when they did, but he was disturbed by Terri's actions. There must have been some connection between them and the raid. But how could she have known? What were her clues? What did she know about drugs? The questions haunted him.

Kurt asked to see the principal, and when asked his reason, he merely said, "I need to interview him for a story in the *Clarion*."

The secretary came back shortly with the message, "Mr. Black can give you ten minutes right away."

Kurt was led into the inner office, and Mr. Black motioned for him to sit down while he finished a phone call.

"Now, what can I do for you," Mr. Black said, putting down the phone.

"I'm Kurt Lang, a reporter on the *Clarion* staff," he began.

"Oh, yes. I'm acquainted with your name. I do read the school paper, you know," he said with a wink.

"We want your reaction to the story in the Sunday paper about the drug raid at the Hagens'. Since it involves some of your students, you must have an opinion."

"Well, I can tell you I was as shocked as

anyone else by the story," he said, leaning back in his leather swivel chair. "I had no idea there was a drug problem in our community. In fact, I'm not sure there is. I think some over-zealous cop wanted to make a name for himself. I've been getting calls all morning from irate parents assuring me their kids were not involved. They resent the fact that Willard High has been given this type of bad publicity."

"You are saying that you do not believe there is a drug problem at Willard. Is that right?" Kurt asked in his best reporter's voice.

"I've been principal here for almost twenty-five years, and I have never had to expel a student because of drugs. We pride ourselves in having a community of kids with high moral standards, and I can't believe any of our kids would get hooked on drugs. Of course, there are always those who come here from some big city and bring their drugs with them, but they soon find out they are in the minority, and out of step with the other kids in the community."

"Then you have no reason to suspect Jim Hagen as a drug user? It was his party, you know."

"I certainly do not. Jim is a fine, outstanding boy—good athlete and good student, and comes from an outstanding home."

"Well, thank you, Mr. Black," Kurt said,

getting up. "I appreciate your time."

"Not at all, son," Mr. Black said. "If you want to know anything else, just call upon me."

"I'll remember that," Kurt said as he left the office. He hoped Mr. Black hadn't detected the sarcasm in his voice.

Kurt couldn't believe what he had just heard. It was almost exactly as Steve had predicted. Even Kurt knew the community wasn't as pure as that. He had been offered drugs a number of times during his school years—once right in the cafeteria.

Kurt went to his fourth hour class, then to lunch. Terri was waiting at a table as usual. After the way she had looked and acted that morning, he wasn't sure she would be there. As he sat down, he noticed that she was still pale, but at least she didn't look like she had been crying any more.

"I suppose I should thank you," he said as he sat down.

"For what?"

"You know, for getting me out of the party before the raid."

"It's all my fault," she said. "We never should have gone to the party. I'm the one who suggested it."

"How could you have known?" Kurt said.

She was silent.

"What I want to know is how you knew it was coming. Who tipped you off?"

"Woman's intuition, I guess," she said.

"It's got to be more than that. You knew . . . some way."

"Please don't press me," Terri said, looking once again as if she were about to cry. "Just be thankful we got away."

"I've been asked to do a story on the raid for the *Clarion*. Will you help me?"

"Please don't," Terri said, reaching across the table and placing her hand on his.

"Why not? It's a perfectly good story."

"You might get hurt," Terri said, pleading.

"You're the second one who's warned me about that today. What do you think, that there is some kind of an underworld here in Twin Falls?"

But Terri didn't answer because some other kids sat down at the table, and the talk drifted to other things.

That night Kurt brought up the subject of drugs at the dinner table. It was one of those rare nights when both he and his father were home for dinner, so Mr. Lang had grilled some steaks, and Kurt had made a salad.

"Dad, what do you know about drugs at our school?" he said after they began eating. "Have you heard of any problems?"

"Our firm doesn't get involved in any juvenile cases," he said. "Most of our work is with corporations, but I do know there is some concern about drugs coming into the community."

"I suppose you saw that they raided a party Friday night at the Hagens'."

"Yes, I did," Mr. Lang said with a chuckle. "And it's kinda ironic. Hagen has been giving advice to everyone else on how to run their families—now he's got this on his hands."

"I think you should know I was there," Kurt said, looking at his dad's face for a reaction.

"At the raid?" he said, without changing expression.

"No, we left before that," Kurt answered.

"Did you see anything?" Mr. Lang asked.

"No. That's the funny part. I never saw anything suspicious. Am I so naive that I don't know what to look for?"

"In a way, I'm glad you're that naive," Mr. Lang said. "It means you haven't been using drugs without me knowing it. I guess I've never worried about it. I just assumed I could trust you. But I really should have given you more help in knowing what to look out for."

"Don't worry, Dad. I'm all right. It's just that I have to do this story on the raid for the *Clarion*, and I'm at a loss to know where to begin."

"Why don't you go to the authorities and see if

you can get some material for your article. I know there is a Sergeant Larson who has been assigned to a new drug unit. I've met him a couple of times, and he seems to be the sort of guy who would be helpful. Give him a call in the morning and ask for an interview."

"Care if I use your name?" Kurt asked.

"If you need to, go ahead," his dad answered.

"Thanks, Dad. I'll let you know how it turns out."

Kurt called Sergeant Larson from the *Clarion* office the following morning and agreed to meet him at 4:30 that afternoon. So, instead of waiting for the bus, Kurt got a ride home with a friend who was driving. He picked up his car and went directly to the police station.

At the station, Kurt was shown to Sergeant Larson's office by a woman at the combination switchboard and radio dispatch desk. This was the first time Kurt had been to the police station, so he was a little taken back by the austerity of it all. Even Larson's office was really just a desk in one corner of a larger room with portable dividers around it. His desk was piled high with papers, and barely visible under the pile was a telephone.

Larson, dressed in sport shirt and jeans, stood up when Kurt entered the room.

"You're the reporter who called me this morning?" he asked.

"That's right," Kurt said, shaking his hand. "I'm Kurt Lang from the *Clarion*."

"And I'm Larson. Don't let these clothes throw you," he said sitting down. "In our work, the less we look like a cop, the better we can do our work. You say you're doing a story for the school paper?"

"You're acquainted with the *Clarion*?" Kurt asked.

"I try to keep up on what's happening at school, and so I read it each week."

"Well, we all know there was a drug raid over the weekend which involved some of our students. I've been assigned to do a story on it, and since I can't find out much around school, I came directly to you."

"I may have to answer 'no comment' to your questions, but I'll do the best I can," Larson said.

"Is it true that your office raided a party at the Hagens' as reported in the daily paper?"

"Yes, that is a matter of record."

"What led you to suspect drugs were being used at the party?"

"We were tipped off by a phone call."

"Did you find any?"

"I can only say that we found enough evidence to bring several students in for questioning," the Sergeant said.

"That was reported in the paper," Kurt said.

72

"Can you tell me their names?"

"No, since they're juveniles, we can't release names."

"Tell me, Sergeant, for my own information, how can you tell if someone has been using drugs?"

"Sometimes it's difficult to tell, and it varies with the drug being used, but if some kid really gets spaced out you can probably tell from his or her dilated eyes and erratic behavior. The best long term evidence is a personality change—a change of attitude toward school and life. The kid often becomes listless, and there is a loss of appetite. I've seen an "A" student one semester almost flunk out the next because of drugs. They don't refer to it as a 'mind controlling substance' for nothing."

"What will happen to the ones you called in for questioning?"

"They were all questioned and released to their parents. If we find that we have enough evidence to convict them, we'll set a trial date, and if convicted, they will probably be sent to a juvenile center where they can get some help with their drug problem. In most cases it's hard to convict. What we want is to find out where they are getting it. Out there somewhere is an adult pusher who is making a good living off those kids. He doesn't care if they are ruined for life—he just wants to make money and support his own habit. He's the one we really want to find and convict."

"Would you say there is a drug problem at Willard High?"

"If one student is using drugs, we consider it a problem," Sergeant Larson said. "But if you mean, is there a widespread use, no. We have no evidence that there is anything more than a minority using them, but we want to stop it before it grows. A community usually only wakes up to the problem when it's too late."

"What are your greatest problems in drug control?" Kurt asked.

"Probably our biggest problem is people not thinking there can be a problem. I've already had some calls yesterday and today from parents who are threatening to sue for damaging their reputation because we took their kids in for questioning. Instead of helping us, the parents immediately become defensive. We need more public awareness of the problems associated with drugs. If you want a focus for your story, why not use that? It would be of great help to the school and the community."

"Thanks, Sergeant," Kurt said, getting to his feet. "You've been extremely helpful. Good luck in finding that pusher."

That evening Kurt had just settled down at his desk to begin writing his story when he heard the phone ring. In a few moments, his dad called up the stairs, "It's for you."

Kurt bounded down the steps, thinking it might be Terri. "Hello," he said in a cheery voice.

"What are you trying to do, play hero?" a male voice said.

"What? What are you talking about?" Kurt stammered in surprise.

"You know what I'm talking about. You tipped off the police Friday night."

"Me? Say, who is this?" Kurt demanded.

"I invite you to a party, and that's the thanks I get."

Now Kurt recognized the voice of Jim Hagen.

"Cool down, Jim," Kurt demanded. "I did not call the police, and I don't know who did. I didn't even know about it until I got to school on Monday morning."

"That's a lie, and you know it," Jim said, his voice getting louder. "Why weren't you there when the police came? I even saw your car at the police station this afternoon—you little stool pigeon."

"If you don't believe me, ask Steve and Nancy. They're the ones who told me about it," Kurt said, trying to defend himself.

"If you know what's good for you, you'll keep out of this and not write your story. If not, you'll find that holy nose of yours flattened all over your goody-goody face." And with that he hung up.

Kurt stood holding the phone in stunned silence.

"Problem?" his father said, coming into the living room from the den.

"You heard?" Kurt said, sitting down.

"I heard enough," his dad said. "Who was it?"

"I'm sure it was Jim Hagen," Kurt answered.

"Don't let him scare you. If you believe in something it may cost you. On the other hand, you had better be extra careful for a while . . . especially if you are out at night. Some people will do anything to protect their drug business. I'll stay out of it, but if you need some legal advice, I can get one of our lawyers to help you."

"But, Dad, he threatened me!"

"There must be someone pushing him," his dad said. "I suspect the dealer he's getting his drugs from would like to see your story stopped."

Kurt went back to his room, but found it impossible to do any studying or writing the remainder of the evening. Even after he went to bed, he tossed nervously for a long time before going to sleep.

Kurt avoided Cindy as much as possible on Monday and Tuesday because he knew exactly what she would say, and she didn't disappoint him.

"I warned you," she said, as they met on the sidewalk on the way to the bus.

"I knew you were going to say that," Kurt said.

"Can you blame me?"

"No, but I'm not sorry that I went."

"How can you say that?" she said, surprised.

"In the first place I was gone before the raid, and in the second place, I've learned more about drugs and people in the last three days than at any time in my life. I just hope I can write the story that needs to be written about it."

"What ever happened to my meek, anti-social neighbor?" Cindy asked.

"He grew up and became a tiger," Kurt said, laughing.

"Just so he doesn't meet someone who's on a safari," she answered as they boarded the bus.

THE PRICE OF A CRUSADE

Kurt's story appeared in the Friday edition of the *Clarion* just prior to Christmas vacation. Although he hadn't planned it that way, it worked out well. It would be two weeks before he had to face anyone at school again.

The story had appeared in spite of the threats. Not only did Kurt get the call from Jim, but there had been calls to other members of the *Clarion* staff, as well as an anonymous letter asking that the story be dropped. There had been a staff meeting in which it was unanimously decided to go ahead with the story, placing special emphasis upon the information which Kurt had received from Sergeant Larson concerning the detection of drug usage. Kurt had ended his story with an appeal for everyone in the school and the community to become aware of the possible problem, and to help keep drugs out of the community.

In the year-end edition of the *Twin Falls Daily*, the drug raid was listed as one of the significant news stories of the previous year. Along with that article, Kurt's story in the *Clarion* was quoted at length.

Suddenly, it seemed everyone was interested in drugs. At the New Year's Eve party at church, Kurt was deluged with questions about it. At church the next Sunday, the pastor mentioned it in his sermon, and a number of people talked to Kurt about it after church.

And in the next few weeks, he found himself in the midst of a crusade against drugs. He hadn't planned it that way, and he didn't exactly enjoy the publicity, but he felt for the first time he was doing something useful with his life.

A committee was formed at school to help educate the students about drugs, and through Kurt's contacts with Sergeant Larson, he was able to get the police to present an assembly program on it. Kurt was asked to lead a discussion on drugs at his youth group meeting, and sat on a panel to discuss drugs at the local Kiwanis Club meeting. He suspected his dad had something to do with that invitation.

After Jim's call, he and Kurt had totally

avoided each other. If Jim saw Kurt coming down the hall, he would turn the other way so he wouldn't have to talk to him. Kurt received a couple of other crank calls, but neither one sounded like Jim. He had become more careful about being home alone, and especially of driving alone at night. But as the weeks went by, the threats died down and so did Kurt's fear.

The investigation into the Hagen party seemed to run into a dead-end with no one being convicted, and no new information appearing in the paper. Kurt suspected that Hagen's money and power in the community had something to do with the way the story was hushed.

During this time, Kurt's relationship with Terri seemed to reach a plateau. They continued to see each other at school, and talk on the phone occasionally, but it wasn't developing into the relationship he had wanted.

Terri and Jan had gone to Texas for the two weeks of Christmas vacation and after Christmas—especially after Kurt became so involved with the drug crusade—Terri seemed to become cool toward him, almost as if she were afraid to be seen with him. She still spent a lot of time with Cindy, and went to some church functions with her, but Kurt and Terri were never alone.

Terri was still the only girl Kurt had any

interest in dating, and he still longed to be with her and to get to know her better. He was also becoming increasingly conscious of his obligation to witness to her. Something seemed to be lacking in her life. She was beautiful, talented, and, at times, loving, but her life seemed unfulfilled.

Kurt decided to try a new approach to their relationship. He had worked many extra hours during Christmas vacation, and had some extra spending money. So after clearing a date with Terri, he made reservations at one of the better restaurants in a downtown hotel. It was noted for its fine dining, and relaxed atmosphere.

Kurt picked her up at the agreed time, and when Terri opened the door, he gave a low whistle.

"Why, thank you," she purred. The longer she lived in Twin Falls, the less she had of her southern accent, but tonight she sounded just like the first time Kurt had met her.

"Do you realize those are the first words I ever heard you say?" Kurt said.

"That seems like a long time ago," Terri answered with a sigh.

Kurt was dressed in a navy blazer, gray slacks, white shirt and red print tie, and she was wearing a light gray suit with a red blouse. This was no accident. She had phoned to ask what he was wearing. It was obvious to Kurt that she had even had her hair done professionally for the occasion.

"Oh, here are some flowers for you," Kurt said, handing her a box.

"How sweet," she responded, giving him a little peck on the cheek. "You know, this is my first corsage."

"Really?"

"I told you, I came from the other side of the tracks."

"Well, come on, for one night let's move to the other side," Kurt said, helping her on with her coat.

As they were about to leave, Jan came into the room. "You two have a good time," she said.

"I will. I don't know about Kurt," Terri replied, taking Kurt's arm.

"I'll leave a light on," Jan said, "just in case you decide you want to come in and talk for a little while."

The evening went well. The dinner was excellent, and the waiter, sensing their desire to be alone, took plenty of time between courses. In the glow of the candlelight, Terri was even more beautiful than she was in the daylight.

They talked about a lot of things—school, friends, music—but as Kurt thought about it later that evening, he realized that most of their discussion had been quite superficial. He was never able to get beneath the surface, nor was he able to open up to her and discuss spiritual things.

When they finished eating, Kurt suggested a movie, but Terri said, "Why don't we just go home and talk some more. It's quieter there."

So Kurt paid the check, and she took his arm. As they walked back through the hotel lobby on the way to the parking ramp, Kurt wished some of his buddies who had thought he would never date could see him now.

For the first time in several weeks, Kurt walked to his car without nervously looking around to see if someone was waiting in the shadows. He suddenly felt free from the fear which had dogged his steps since that first threat. But, if he had been more careful, he would have seen a car, parked across the street from the hotel, pull out of its parking spot as he left the ramp and follow at a safe distance all the way to Terri's house.

They got back to the house about 10:30 p.m., and Jan had apparently already retired. The light in the living room was on dim, and there were some dishes of nuts and candies scattered around on the tables.

"Well, I've been a gentleman as long as I can," Kurt said, taking off his coat and tie.

"I guess this is about my limit, too," Terri said, kicking off her heels, and removing her earrings. They both sat down on the davenport. Terri pulled her legs up under her, and leaned over against Kurt. He reached out and put his arm around her.

"This is better than talking," he whispered.

"But we really should talk," Terri said. "We haven't done much of that lately."

"That's not my fault," Kurt answered.

Terri was quiet for a little while, and then said, "No, I guess I'm the one who has kept my distance while you've been on this drug crusade."

"That's what I can't understand about you," Kurt said. "At times, like tonight, you seem so warm and loving, and at other times, so strange, so distant, as if you were in another world."

"Maybe I am," Terri said.

"What do you mean?" Kurt asked.

"Just that . . . at times, I may be in another world from yours. We do live in two different worlds, you know."

"Are our worlds that different?" Kurt asked.

Terri sat up so she could look directly into Kurt's face. "Kurt, I've seen life from a different perspective than you have. I told you I grew up in a home where just about everything was okay. I've seen my mother and father drunk and stoned out of their minds, and I've watched my mother bring home boyfriends for the night without so much as an explanation to me.

"And then," she continued, "I came here to live with Jan. She's as pure and holy as they come. I've never even seen her get mad. She's always been kind to my mother, even when my mother used her terribly. And Jan says this is because she has Christ in her heart. I'm not sure what all that means.

"And you and Cindy seem to be part of her world. You see everything so black and white. I tend to see everything gray. I've grown up to believe that anything can be okay in its proper context. I've been taught to lie if it's for your ultimate good, and cheat if you know you won't get caught."

Kurt was beginning to feel uncomfortable. This was a different Terri than he had ever seen before, and his feelings were being torn apart. On the one hand, his heart went out in love to the beautiful girl sitting beside him. He longed to reach out and take her into his arms. But, on the other hand, this was a stranger talking to him . . . a stranger whose words and actions did not fit into his concept of what was right or fair, and he was repulsed by what he was hearing.

She lay her head back on his shoulder, and they were silent again for a few minutes. Then he thought he heard her begin to cry. He reached over and lifted her chin with one hand and looked into her eyes. Sure enough, there were big tears beginning to form.

"Terri, why are you crying?"

She didn't answer.

"See, there you go again—sweet and lovely one minute, and a total stranger the next."

"I can't help it," she said, sobbing lightly. "It's just that no one ever treated me like you do. Every guy I've ever met wanted something from me—not me. But you seem to want me, and if you really knew what I'm like you wouldn't."

"But I care about you, Terri." Kurt was surprised to hear the words coming from his lips. "I care very much."

"How can you say that when you don't know me?" she said.

"Let's just say, I love the part I know—a beautiful, wonderful girl."

"But I'm not a beautiful person, believe me," she said, sitting up and blowing her nose.

"I think I had better be going," Kurt said, getting up.

"Don't go . . . not yet," she pleaded, trying to pull him down.

"I have to go home. School tomorrow, you know."

"I know, but just don't go."

"Terri, what's gotten into you? One minute . . . oh, well, we've been through that before. I'm going." And with that, he picked up his coat and tie and started for the door.

She got up and followed him, and he saw that

she was trembling. He could resist her no longer. He took her in his arms, and kissed her tenderly and long. When he finally released her, he turned quickly and opened the door. As he left, he heard her say, "Be careful, Kurt. Please be careful," but he didn't stop to ask what she meant.

Kurt took out his keys to unlock his car door, but just as he did so, two figures came out of the shadows and grabbed him from behind. He tried to cry out, but found a big hand clamped across his mouth. One of the figures pulled Kurt's arms behind him, and whirled him around. Then Kurt felt the stinging blow of knuckles across his face. Twice more the blows came, each time harder, and by that time his knees began to buckle. As he was going down, he heard a man's voice say, "That should keep his mouth shut for a little while."

The next thing he knew, he was lying on the davenport in Jan's house, and she was applying cold towels to his face which was beginning to swell. Terri was sitting on the floor beside him, crying uncontrollably. He tried to speak, but found that his lips were swollen too badly to be able to form any words.

His mind was beginning to clear when his dad arrived. From the conversation, Kurt knew Jan had called him. After examining Kurt to see how badly he was hurt, his dad went to the phone and called the police and an ambulance. The police came, but there was little they could do until Kurt could tell them what had happened, so they took him to the emergency room at the hospital.

Kurt's upper lip and right cheek were cut badly and required a number of stitches, but the x-rays showed no broken bones, and his father was able to take him home that night.

It was 4:00 a.m. when his dad helped him into bed and gave him some pain pills which the doctor had sent along. As Kurt began to doze off, he could still hear, "Be careful, Kurt. Please be careful."

And now he knew what she had meant.

SPRING GROWTH

Kurt missed about ten days of school. When he did go back, his stitches were out, and the swelling gone, but there were still some bright red streaks where the cuts had been, and black and blue marks on his forehead and cheeks.

The police had asked many questions, but since he had not seen his assailants, and could not give a description of a car, there was little the police could do. Sergeant Larson was convinced it was related to Kurt's part in the crusade against drugs, and Jim Hagen was his number one suspect because of the threatening phone call, but there was no hard evidence that could bring about an arrest.

Cindy came over every day after school to fill Kurt in on what was happening at church and school, and she even shuttled assignments back and forth between Kurt and his teachers. Kurt kept waiting for her to say, "I warned you," but she didn't and seemed genuinely concerned about him.

In one of her early visits she did ask, "Do you think Jim did it?"

"I really don't know," Kurt answered. "There were two of them, and the one voice which I did hear was not Jim's."

"But how did they know you were there?" she asked.

"I don't know that either, except that Jim would know my car."

"Could they have been tipped off?" she asked.

Kurt was lying on the davenport, and turned his eyes away from Cindy and to the ceiling. "I like to think not," he said, "but Terri's warning before I went outdoors makes me suspicious."

"That little snake!" Cindy said emphatically. "How could she do it?"

"We don't know she did," Kurt said, "and I would like to give her the benefit of the doubt. How could anyone so lovely and so sweet do anything like that?"

"You sure are blind . . . or in love," Cindy said.

"Maybe both," Kurt answered, "but we have to keep in touch with her. How else can we witness to her?"

"I'm not sure that is your major motive," Cindy answered.

"Sometimes motives become blurred when you care about someone," Kurt said, and then quickly changed the subject.

The story of the assault had made all of the papers, so Kurt was something of a hero when he returned to school. It seemed that everyone wanted to talk to him about it—everyone that is, except Jim Hagen, who kept his distance from Kurt, and Terri, who once again seemed uneasy around him.

Terri had called several times during the time Kurt was at home, but she never offered to come over. And, since Kurt was still sorting out his feelings for her, he did not encourage her calls.

Even Mr. Black called Kurt to the office, and thanked him for his part in alerting the community to a drug problem. "I am pleased by the way our school and community has responded to this problem," he said. "We all knew there was a problem, but it took this incident to bring it out into the open."

Kurt wanted to remind him of his earlier conversation, but merely said, "Thanks for your help, Mr. Black," and left the room.

That might have been the end of Terri and Kurt's relationship, but every time he saw her, he fell in love with her all over again. And as time passed, he rationalized away any part she might have had in his beating, and began to date her again. He would come away from some dates feeling he had made progress, but then something would happen to put their relationship back to zero. But about a month before graduation, he sensed a change in her attitude. Kurt first noticed it one Saturday early in May.

It was the first warm day of the year. The temperature was up into the 70's, and the green grass was beginning to push up through the dead leaves. Kurt had called Terri on Friday night to see if she wanted to play tennis on Saturday. She had started to work in a local restaurant, and he agreed to pick her up when she got off work at 3:00 p.m.

Kurt worked around the house that morning, and after lunch put on some white tennis shorts, carefully selecting socks and a red shirt that also matched the red stripes on his Nikes. When he was finally dressed, he took a long look at himself in the mirror. His face was almost back to normal now, and he had grown almost three inches during his senior year. His hair was darker because of the long winter indoors, but he knew a few days in the sun would bring it back to normal again.

It was about a quarter to three when he pulled up in front of Terri's restaurant, and waited for her to come out. About one minute after three, she came running out the side door, and in one move, opened the door and jumped in beside Kurt.

"Hi, handsome," she said, looking him up and down.

"Hello, beautiful," he responded. "You look good even in that brown waitress uniform."

Terri leaned over and gave Kurt a kiss on the cheek.

"Is that all I get for picking you up?" he said, pretending to pout.

"Never satisfied!" she said, winking. "All of this attention lately has gone to your head. Come on, let's go to my house so I can change. I want to deflate your ego by beating you on the court today."

They drove to Terri's house and went inside. Jan was in the kitchen, so Kurt went in there to wait while Terri went upstairs to change.

"Well, you look like summer," Jan said, while stirring some cake batter.

"It's May," Kurt said. "It should start warming up soon."

"I've known summer to wait until July around here," she said. "I never did figure out why I left Texas to come north."

"I guess I didn't know you were from Texas, too," Kurt said, pulling up a stool and sitting where he could watch Jan.

"Sure. Terri's mother and I were both born and raised in Texas, but I fell in love with a soldier boy who was stationed down there, and told him I would follow him to the ends of the world. Well, this isn't quite it, but you can see it from here."

"What happened?" Kurt asked.

"I was just 17 and he was 19. We thought we were deeply in love. And I guess we were, but we just didn't know what all was involved. We didn't know that love carried with it some responsibilities. We drove up here to visit his folks on a two week leave with the idea of getting married before it was over, but he was called back suddenly, and we never went through with it."

"And you stayed here?" Kurt asked.

"I didn't even have enough money to go back home. His folks took me in like their own daughter. He was an only child, so I guess I became the daughter they had always wanted."

Jan put the cake in the oven, and pulled up a stool beside Kurt.

"What about your parents? I'm 17, and I can't imagine what my dad would say if I told him I was going to get married," Kurt said.

"Oh, my parents didn't know where I was for a long time. You see, they moved around a lot in the south, and finally my sister and I decided we had moved enough, so we stayed in Dallas

96

while they moved on. We heard from them occasionally, but from the day they left, they never gave us another dime. We worked for everything we had.

"But I suppose you really want to know what happened to my soldier boy," she continued. "He had orders to go to Viet Nam, and that's the last I ever saw of him."

"You mean he was killed?" Kurt asked.

"No, that would have been easier for me to take. He wrote a lot at first, and then the letters became fewer and fewer. He sent some money home at first, too, but soon quit answering my letters and those of his parents. He spent two years in Nam, and when he returned, he called me from New York and wanted me to come out there and live. He still didn't know what he wanted to do, so I suggested he find some work, and then send for me. That's the last I ever heard of him."

"What about his folks?"

"It nearly broke their hearts. They were the kindest, sweetest people I have ever known. I continued to live with them, and took care of them until they both died. They made up to me for everything my parents didn't do. This was their house, you know. They left everything they had to me."

"Wow, what a story!" Kurt exclaimed. "Sounds straight from the soaps."

"I learned a lot from that experience. I found out you need to really know someone before you marry them." She reached over and patted Kurt's hand. "Take it from me, be sure you know someone—really know her—before you decide to spend the rest of your life with her."

Kurt wondered if Jan sensed how hard it had been for him to get to know Terri. In fact, he wondered if her little speech wasn't for his benefit.

"The Lord has been good to me," she said thoughtfully as she looked out the window. "The Lord has a way of making things work out for His good. If I hadn't come here I may never have become a Christian. You see, Jesse's parents were Christians, and they began taking me to church with them, and that is where I found Christ."

"I'm ready," Terri said, coming into the kitchen.

"Far out!" Kurt exclaimed and gave a whistle. Terri had changed into a blue tennis outfit and had tied her hair in a pony tail so it hung down the middle of her back like a long shiny rope.

"Don't wait dinner," Terri said. "I have a feeling this might be a long afternoon."

"You kids have a good time," Jan said, giving Kurt a little hug.

"Hey, how about me," Terri said. "I'm your kid,

too, you know."

"You, I can hug anytime," Jan said, laughing. "It isn't often I get to hug a handsome boy like this."

"Careful, he gets a big head easily," Terri said.

As Terri and Kurt walked out to the car, Kurt said, "Wow, she is something else! I wish she were my mother."

"I guess I'm pretty lucky to have her. I used to feel sorry for myself because I had such a poor mother, but I guess Jan has made up for it."

They got into the car and drove off. After they had gone a few blocks, Terri said, "You know, I won't be living with Jan much longer."

"Why?" Kurt asked, so surprised he almost ran a red light.

"I'm going back to Texas after I graduate," she said.

"But why? You've got nothing there and everything here. You've got Jan, and me. What about me?" Kurt was driving almost blindly now.

"I'm sorry it had to come out like it did. I've been meaning to tell you but I've kept putting it off. You see, I promised my mother I would come back and live with her after I got through school. I'm really torn, because things are so much better here, but she is my mother, and I do feel sorry for her. I guess I can't expect Jan to support me all my life."

"But Jan doesn't want you to leave, does she?" Kurt asked.

"No. She has even said she would put me through college," Terri answered. "She's got plenty of money, and would like to have me stay here to keep her company. She's a lonely woman . . . but so is my mother. There are so many lonely people in the world."

"After everything you've told me about your background, I just can't understand why you would want to go back to it," Kurt said.

"It's hard to explain," Terri said. "I know this is a better world, but it's not my world. These months have been like a beautiful vacation in another land, but all vacations have to come to an end, and at some point you have to go home."

"But this is one time you can stay in paradise."

"Are you saying you want me to stay?" Terri asked.

Kurt glanced over and saw that Terri was looking intently at him, but he quickly looked back to the road because they were in traffic now.

"Sure, I want you to stay," Kurt answered. "Haven't I made that obvious? Have I even looked at another girl since you moved in?"

"No, but Cindy tells me that you didn't look at

anybody before I moved in either," Terri said.

"So, you've been talking to Cindy again," Kurt said.

"Well, I had to have some idea of how serious you were, so I asked Cindy. She seems to know you better than anyone else."

"And what did she say?"

"She said that any girl who could make you fall in love deserves a medal. She said she had tried for years, but gave up."

"She said that! I told you she was like a sister to me."

"But even sisters need love," Terri said. "She thinks a lot of you and would have loved you if you had given her half a chance. You can play that game with her, but I need to know where I stand. I've seen too much with my father, and Jan's soldier boyfriend. I want all or nothing."

By this time they were at the tennis courts, and got out of the car without continuing the subject. One court was open, so they went in and immediately began to play. Ordinarily, Kurt would have been highly competitive and would have beaten Terri badly, but today, he was quiet, and did poorly, missing shots left and right.

"Oh, come on, Kurt, you're not even trying," Terri called from across the court.

"Maybe my mind isn't on the game," Kurt said.

"Well, get it on the game, or let's stop playing," Terri said as she sent a serve right past Kurt.

"Maybe we need to talk more than play," Kurt said.

They put their rackets back into the car, locked it, and began to walk toward the lake in the middle of the park. It was a beautiful day. The sun was warm, and bicycles, kids and dogs were everywhere.

Kurt reached out and put his arm around Terri's waist, and she responded by doing the same, but they continued to walk in silence. When they got to the far side of the lake, where there were fewer people, they sat down on the grass.

"Wish we'd brought a blanket," Kurt said. "This grass is going to stain our clothes."

"They'll wash," Terri said, pushing Kurt back on the grass. She followed, and lay on her stomach close beside him looking down into his eyes.

"Now, what about that talking you wanted to do?" she said.

Kurt continued to stare past Terri into the sky. A couple of birds were drifting back and forth, and the whole world seemed at peace—so different from the storm which was raging in his heart and mind.

"Terri, I don't want you to go, you know that.

Ever since that day when you walked onto our bus, I've wanted you, and wanted to get to know you better. You don't know what I went through to get you to notice me."

"So, I've noticed. Why haven't you done more about it?"

"More? What could I do more? Terri, I've tried to love you, but every time we get close, you seem to back off like a child touching a hot stove. Growing up without a mother around the house, I must have missed something about women. I don't know what you expect."

"I want to know I'm more than just an object," Terri said. "So many guys have treated me like a thing . . . a big doll to play with. But I'm for real. I hurt. I feel. I'm not sure you do. Sometimes I think you're more interested in trying to make me into a Christian than you are in me . . . for me."

They were silent.

"I'm sorry I've hurt you, Kurt. This had the promise of being such a great afternoon, and now I've spoiled everything."

"You haven't spoiled it, but the things you said today . . . the way Cindy sees me . . . the way you see me, paints a totally different picture of me than I've ever known, and it's a little hard to accept."

"Again, I say, I'm sorry. Maybe it is better that I'm going away," Terri said, sitting up.

"Don't say that," Kurt said, also sitting up. "Give me a chance to show you that I love you. I promise I'll do my best."

"There's only a month left, you know," Terri answered.

"I know . . . I know," he said, getting up.

GRADUATION PARTY— CHURCH STYLE

Kurt lay awake for several hours that night. The day had started out so great, and it had been good—up to a point. But somehow his conversation with Terri seemed so unfinished. It had left him with more questions than it had answered.

There seemed to be no question that she liked him. The fact that she had asked Cindy about him proved that. And he was confident that he cared deeply about her. But how could he express that?

On the one hand, she seemed to be suggesting that he hadn't gone far enough with her, but on the other hand it seemed she was suggesting a different quality of love—something he didn't have.

He had developed some rather definite opinions about pre-marital sex, and had been satisfied with his stand. Some of his feelings on the issue certainly came from church. There he had heard over and over again how wrong it was. And his father, though not a Christian, held some rather strong moral and ethical views concerning sex. In the law office, he had seen the results of disobedience to both the laws of God and man.

So Kurt had been able to handle his sexual drives without much problem up to this time. But as he lay on his bed that night, he began to question what he really did believe. Maybe this was what Terri was suggesting. And the thought of having sex with Terri seemed very different from locker-room talk. He had read some books where sex was presented as the natural expression of two people's love for each other.

Maybe love was the key . . . the difference. If he really loved Terri, maybe the best way he could show her was through sex. Would this convince her that he could and did really love her? If so, he didn't have much time to prove it.

Sometime during that night a plan began to develop. He would find some place and time to prove his love for her. He would have to make a time when they could be alone for a while without interruption. And he had to do it soon, or she would be gone . . . maybe forever.

The first possibility of such a meeting came when Brad and Cindy began talking about a graduation party at church. It was meant to honor the graduates from the church, but was open to anyone from the high school who wished to attend. It had been well-planned and advertised, and Kurt was surprised at the number of people who were planning to come. It was to be a semi-formal dinner at a motel banquet room with a well-known pro football player as the speaker.

Cindy and Brad brought the subject up again for the umpteenth time at lunch one day, and as Terri and Kurt walked back to class, Terri said, "What do you think? Should we go?"

"I hadn't thought much about it, but it's up to you," Kurt said, rather surprised that Terri would bring it up.

"Well, I think we should, even if it's just for Cindy and Brad's sake. Cindy has been a real friend to me, and I won't be seeing her much more. Besides, it sure would make Jan happy. She has been hinting about it for a couple of months now. Let's talk about it after school," she called back to him from down the hall.

This was one move Kurt had not expected. He

certainly wasn't opposed to the idea, but a little surprised. Somehow he had never thought of asking Terri to go because he assumed she wouldn't want to. Now he was embarrassed that he hadn't taken the initiative.

"So, what did you decide?" Terri asked as they walked to the bus after school.

"I told you that I didn't care," Kurt said. "Just so it doesn't take the place of the graduation night party."

"You sound like you have plans for it," she teased.

"Sure, don't you?" Kurt answered.

"Just so we have the same plans," Terri said.

Kurt smiled as he thought about how true he hoped those words really were.

And there was another surprising twist to the church party. Terri suggested to Cindy that they double for the night. So, since he was driving, and Cindy lived next door, Kurt picked her up first that night.

"Thanks for going," Cindy said after she got into the car.

"How did you manage this?" Kurt asked.

"I didn't manage anything," Cindy protested. "It was all Terri's idea."

"Sure. After you had been pressuring her for a month."

"I did not pressure her, and besides it won't

hurt either of you. Who knows? You might enjoy it."

"Just remember, I wouldn't be doing this if it weren't for Terri," Kurt said.

"I know. Don't rub it in," Cindy said.

"What did you mean by that?" Kurt asked.

"Never mind, you wouldn't understand. Just head for Brad's house."

They picked up Brad, and then went to Terri's place. They were at the motel by 6:30 p.m., so they had plenty of time to sit in the lobby and talk before it began.

Kurt was amazed at the number of kids who were there . . . some he had never expected to see at a church party. He wondered why some of them had come because he was confident they had stopped for a beer or two on the way. He decided that many had probably come because of the popularity of the speaker.

The thing that really amazed Kurt was how well Terri seemed to be adapting to the situation. She seemed happier than he had ever known her. The four sat at a table for eight, and before long everyone was in a great mood. Even Kurt loosened up and joined the fun.

The food was great and the music contemporary. The program consisted of several musical numbers by members of a Christian musical group, and some funny skits about graduation. Then the speaker was introduced.

Kurt had slid down in his chair, expecting to be bored out of his tree, but after the first five minutes, he was sitting up listening to every word, and he noticed that Terri was doing the same thing. Instead of a sermon, the speaker gave his testimony.

He talked about the crisis points in his life, and how God had met him at each of these points. His first crisis had come when he was a just so-so player, and was struggling to become identified as a pro. He told of reaching the point where he had considered suicide because he was the last one cut from a team. At that point, he heard about Jesus Christ, and asked Christ to give him a reason for living. "Christ became not only my Savior, but also my coach, my helper, and my friend," he said. "Anything I have accomplished in life, on or off the field, I owe to Him."

Then he talked about the crisis of love, and how Christ had given him the capacity to love . . . really love . . . for the first time. And then he talked about the crisis of commitment, and how he had struggled with who and what would be first in his life. He told of coming to the point where he had to say, "Christ, you are number one in my life. Even if this means giving up football, you can be number one." He went on to say that, instead of asking him to give up his sports, Christ had used football in his life as a means of ministry. "For instance," he said, "would you be sitting there listening to me tonight if I hadn't been the number one pass receiver in the league this last year? It is my success at football that makes my message of Christ seem credible to you."

Kurt had never heard a sermon like that. He had been going to church for ten years, but it always seemed the speaker was in another world—a world totally apart from his. But this guy seemed to be a part of the real world.

When the speaker finished, the kids clapped and cheered, whistled, and even stood to their feet. Kurt found himself spontaneously standing and cheering along with the rest. He glanced over and saw that Terri was doing the same.

The party was over by 11:00 p.m., so the four drove around for a little while, and finally found a little cafe where they could get some ice cream before going home. Everyone, including Terri, seemed in a great mood, and Kurt had a good feeling about the evening.

They took Cindy home first, and Kurt waited while Brad took her to the door. When he got back, they teased Brad about how long his good-nights took. Then they took Brad home, and that left Kurt and Terri alone.

"Want to come to my place?" Kurt said. "Dad's away for the weekend."

"What time is it?" Terri asked.

111

Kurt looked at his watch under the light of the dash. "It's just a little after midnight," he answered.

"I think I can be out another hour before Jan begins to worry," Terri said.

Kurt felt himself getting excited. Maybe this would be the break he was looking for.

He let her out of the car, and they walked together to the house. He produced his key and opened the door. She waited while he switched on the light, and then they went into the living room.

Terri sat down on the sofa, and Kurt took off his coat and sat down beside her. He reached over and drew her closer and without hesitation, she put her head on his shoulder.

They were quiet for a little while. Terri seemed deep in thought, while Kurt was considering what moves he should make. Finally Terri said, "What if he's right?"

"Who?" Kurt asked, surprised.

"The speaker."

"Right about what?" Kurt asked, a little disturbed by the turn of the conversation.

"He said Christ can change your life," Terri said.

"Yeah. Guess he did," Kurt said.

"Didn't that get to you?" she asked.

"Was it supposed to?" he answered.

"Kurt Lang," she said straightening up, "how

insensitive can you be? You may not see anything wrong with your life, but others might. I know there's plenty wrong in my life, and if I could be sure that Christ could straighten me out like the man said, I would accept Him in a minute."

Kurt knew this was his golden opportunity to talk to her about Christ, but he just couldn't do it. Instead of jumping at the opportunity, he remained silent. In the days to come he would look back in regret upon this lost moment. In the words of the speaker that night, he dropped the pass while standing in the end zone.

"Don't you ever wonder what would happen if you were to die today?" she continued.

"Sure, I've thought about it, but after I accepted Christ back in junior high, it hasn't worried me. Can't we talk about something else besides dying?" he said, annoyed.

"Sure, it's just that he got me to thinking, and I thought maybe you felt the same way, and we could talk about it. Obviously there are other things on your mind."

"It's just that there's so much else we need to talk about. In a couple of weeks you're going to be gone, and there's so much we haven't settled."

"Like what?" she asked.

"Like, do you love me?" he said.

"That's a hard question to answer," Terri said,

thoughtfully. "I know I care about you more than anyone else at this moment, but I don't know if this is love. I've never really loved anyone before, so I don't have anything to compare it to."

"I love you," Kurt said, drawing her even closer. "I love you so much I'm ready to do anything necessary to prove that it's for real."

Terri was quiet, but relaxed in Kurt's arms. Finally she said, "There was a time when I would have taken you up on that proposition immediately, but tonight it seems different...so out of place. I just don't know."

"Just last week you seemed to be suggesting it," Kurt said.

"I know, but tonight I feel different, especially after listening to that speaker."

"When will you know?" Kurt pressed for an answer.

"I'll know before I leave next week . . . I promise. Either I want you totally, or I will have to go back to Dallas and start a new life without you."

"Don't say that. It sounds so final," he pleaded.

Kurt could tell the conversation had gone about as far as it was going to go that night, so he offered to take her home, and she seemed more than willing to go.

After he had stopped the car at Jan's house, and before he got out to open her door, he said, "Will you promise me something?"

"I'll try," Terri answered.

"By next Friday night, I need to know where we stand. I'll make the time and the place, but you'll have to bring the answer."

"I promise," Terri said.

And with that he took her to the door.

KURT MAKES FINAL PLANS

The location for the graduation party had been selected by a committee of parents, students, and administrators. The site chosen was the YMCA camp just outside the city. It had the perfect facility for a party of about 200. The main lodge was of massive log construction with a rock fireplace at one end that reached from the floor to the ceiling, 30 feet above it.

There was a floor which could be used for dancing, and still leave plenty of lounge area for those who just wanted to sit and talk. Off the main room were several smaller rooms in which games could be set up, and a kitchen large enough and well enough equipped to supply the endless pop, ice cream, and popcorn which it would take to get through the evening.

Another reason for the selection of the site was that it could be made fairly well secure. Once the kids got there, they were to remain until they decided to leave, and then they could not return. This would prevent some from going into town for liquor and then returning to disrupt the party.

The place was acceptable to almost everyone. Many of the kids had gone to camp there as children, and were acquainted with the facilities. For Kurt, the selection had another significance. He had spent the entire previous summer working at the camp, and he knew every inch of the grounds.

It took most of another night to complete his plans, but by morning, he was proud of himself. He decided he would get a key to one of the staff cabins and use it as the place for a rendezvous with Terri. He wasn't sure yet how he would get the key, but he knew his way around the grounds, and he should be able to get it somehow.

His big break came as he was walking down the hall at school one day the following week. He met Tim Hunter, who he knew was on the party committee, and asked, "How are things going with the party?"

"Rotten," Tim answered.

"What's the matter?" Kurt asked.

"Two guys I was banking on helping with the

decorating have just backed out."

"Could I help?" Kurt asked. "I know the facilities better than most of you."

"Wow, that would be great! Would you?"

"I guess I can spare an evening," Kurt said. "Finals will be over by that time."

"Great," Tim answered. "Meet here at the school about 6:30 on Thursday evening, and you can ride out with someone."

Things were going even better than he had hoped. Now he was sure he could get his hands on a key. He knew every cabin, and every key, and knew just where they were kept.

On Thursday evening, Kurt went with five others in a car out to Camp Idahope. Three sets of parents were also there, so the twelve of them set to work transforming the big lodge into a party room with a nautical theme.

As soon as he could do so without being too obvious, Kurt went into the kitchen, and then through a dark hall to the closet which he knew contained the keys to the cabins. Carefully, he tried the knob. He was in luck, the closet was unlocked. It was never locked during the summer season because there was always someone in the lodge, but he hadn't been sure about now. He carefully opened the door, and then closed it behind him before reaching for the cord to turn on the light. He didn't want anyone to see the light and get suspicious.

He pulled the cord, and the small room lit up. It was just as he remembered it. And there on the wall, each on its proper peg, were the keys to the various buildings on the grounds. He knew exactly which one he wanted. He had thought it through the night before, and had decided the nurse's cabin would be best. It was hidden from the view of the lodge, and it contained enough furniture to make it comfortable. Also, it could be locked from the inside. The nurse had insisted on that because she didn't want people walking in on her while she was trying to sleep. If anyone was going to get sick at camp, it usually happened during the night.

Kurt carefully removed one of the two keys from the proper peg, and put it in his pocket. Since there was still another key on the peg, it would be difficult to detect that one was missing unless someone was deliberately looking for it.

He turned off the light, and carefully opened the door so that no one would hear him. Everything seemed to be as before, so he was able to slip back into the main room without anyone noticing him or his absence.

Everyone worked hard that night, and by midnight everything seemed in readiness for the next night's party.

"Better go home and get some sleep," one of the parents said. "After all, you're not going to get any sleep tomorrow night . . . we'll see to that," he said with a wink.

"I wouldn't miss it," Kurt said with a smile on his face, and his hand firmly holding the key in his pocket.

And yet, as he left that night, he had the uneasy feeling that he had done something wrong. Even after he went to bed, he tossed and turned for a long time trying to ease his conscience and rationalize his actions.

CABIN FEVER

"This way," Kurt whispered as they reached the fork in the path.

"Where are we going?" Terri asked, also in a whisper.

"You'll see," Kurt answered.

"Are you sure the sponsors didn't see us?" Terri asked.

"Naw, they're all too busy, and if they did they couldn't find us because they don't know these grounds as well as I do."

"The man of experience!" Terri said, laughing.

Kurt didn't say anything, but wondered if Terri really sensed what little experience he had in this sort of thing.

The moon was full, and as their eyes became accustomed to the darkness, the path ahead became visible. As they reached the cabin, Kurt felt his heart begin to beat faster, and his face flushed. As he reached in his pocket for the key, he found he was trembling. He had a sudden urge to drop the key and run, but then realized his plans had gone too far to back out. The decision had been made, and now he had to live with the results—whatever they might be.

He unlocked the door and motioned for Terri to enter. The moon, shining through the cabin windows, made the room look like something left over from Halloween. The silver rays highlighted the white sheets which had been placed over the chairs and davenport to protect them from dust, and made them look like ghosts standing guard over their haunted house.

When Terri first saw them, she gave a frightened little cry, but Kurt put a reassuring arm around her, and she went with him into the room. He pulled the protective covers off the davenport, and they sat down.

"Do you realize this is the first time we have ever been alone with no curfew?" Kurt began. "For once, we can talk without interruption."

"Is that why you brought me here?" Terri asked.

"Terri, I came here for your answer," Kurt said, trying to draw her closer to himself. "Last week you promised an answer if I made the time and place. Well, we've got the time, and here is the place. Before we leave this cabin, I need to know if you really love me."

"You make it sound so simple," Terri said softly, "but it isn't. I've thought a lot about it this week. Before I came to Twin Falls, I wouldn't have thought twice about hopping in that bed over there to show someone I loved them—or thought I loved them. But with you it seems so different . . . it seems so wrong."

"What's the difference? Am I any less a man?" Kurt asked.

"Not at all," Terri said, straightening up where she could see his face in the moonlight. "Just the opposite. You seem too much of a man to have to resort to sex to prove your love."

"But why do you think I went to all the trouble of getting this place and planning this time together?" Kurt said, sounding annoyed.

"I know, I know," she said. "But I'm not sure that's what you really want. Kurt, take it from me, there are other ways of proving your love. If sex alone meant love, then I would have known love, but I haven't. I started to go with you because I thought maybe you knew something about love that I didn't. Now I see you don't. You've got love and sex all confused like so many others."

"But, Terri, I want you. That's why I brought you here tonight—to teach me something about love."

She was quiet for a moment, and then added,

as if in deep thought, "Funny, isn't it? I've had sex, and didn't find love, and you haven't and still don't know the meaning of love. Doesn't that prove that love is something above and beyond the physical?"

Kurt felt his face begin to flush again. Her words came like stinging indictments. He was becoming angry, but he wasn't sure if it was at Terri or himself. She was beginning to make him and his plans sound so wrong, and yet she had admitted having sex before—apparently many times. What right did she have to judge his actions?

"How do you know I haven't had sex?" Kurt asked.

"I can tell. You're much too . . . too innocent."

"Innocent? You make me sound like a child. Am I being refused because I haven't had enough experience for you?"

"Believe me, Kurt," she said, reaching over and patting his face, "I know the other side. Stay the way you are. The best way I can show my love for you right now is to get out of here before either of us does something to change that innocence. If I stay, all of this big talk of mine will disappear. You are physically attractive to me, but I really do want you to keep your morals intact."

"Terri, don't go. Please," Kurt was pleading now.

Terri was on her feet. "I'm going to leave, and don't follow me. You stay here until I'm gone. You stay the way you are. And me? Well, I'm going back to Dallas. There I don't have to pretend. All the time I've been here with Jan and you and Cindy, I've had to be something I'm really not. I thought for a while all of you could teach me a new way of life ... and once in awhile I've seen what I want as if from the distance ... like the other night listening to that preacher. But now I realize you don't have the answers either. Maybe deep down you're pretending too. Who knows?"

Kurt was on his feet now, and grabbed Terri by the arms. "Maybe I don't know all the answers, but I know I love you. I've loved you since the first day I saw you."

Terri pulled away from his grasp and started backing toward the door. "Look, Kurt, I'm going out that door, and don't try to stop me. If you do, I'll yell, and you'll be in big trouble. Maybe I have learned something during these months after all ... I've learned how to say no. I do love you ... enough to say no. I wish we could have worked it out, but we just can't ...." And with that she opened the door and started to run.

"Terri, please ..." He heard his voice resound in the empty cabin as the clicking of her heels on the sidewalk grew fainter.

Kurt went back to the sofa and sat down. His

mind was about to go into orbit. He was going back and forth from embarrassment to anger and back again. He knew deep down she was right, but he couldn't face it.

And then his anger turned to shame. He had been rebuffed by someone who wasn't even a Christian. It should have been the other way. He should have been the one with the higher standards. She had expected much more from him because he was a Christian, but he had failed her.

Kurt put his head in his hands, and tried to pray, but all that would come out was "Dear God, please help me." Hot tears began to flow from between his fingers, and roll down his arms, and he began to sob as he hadn't done for years.

Eventually Kurt regained his composure and started to walk slowly toward the lodge. Nothing mattered to him any more . . . he didn't even bother to close the cabin door. He didn't care who knew he had been there. He had planned for a graduation that never came off . . . and he was drained emotionally. He suddenly felt very tired, and decided to sit down on a bench within the shadows of the well-house.

In the silence, he could hear a truck shifting gears as it climbed a hill on a nearby freeway, and a dog bark on some nearby farm. But then he heard a car door open, and some voices.

There were other voices in the background coming from the lodge, but these seemed much closer.

His first thought was that another couple was out walking. He didn't want anyone to see him there in the darkness alone, so he stood up and leaned against the well-house where he would be hidden in the shadows. When the voices didn't appear to be coming his way, he moved carefully toward the edge of the building where he could get a better view of the parking lot. The voices seemed to be coming from that direction.

As he peered around the building, he could see two forms standing beside a car. The one looked like a middle-aged man, and, even in the dim light, seemed familiar. Kurt watched until the man turned so that the moonlight fell full on his face, and then Kurt remembered where he had seen him before. It was, without doubt, Chester—the man who had been at Jim Hagen's house the night of the Sadie Hawkins party.

Kurt listened carefully. He heard another voice ask, "Did you bring it?"

"I've got all you can get rid of," the older man said.

"Good, now you just stay by the car and out of sight, and I'll bring the customers to you."

Kurt watched as the second figure turned

around and started toward the lodge. Then Kurt got a glimpse of his face. Now he knew ... the second person was Jim Hagen.

There was no way Kurt could go from the well-house to the lodge without Chester seeing him, so he stood quietly and waited. Soon he heard voices again, and once more positioned himself where he could see as well as hear. Shortly Jim brought a fellow out, and after some low discussion, which Kurt could not hear, he could see the glow of two cigarettes.

So Chester was a pusher! That explained his relationship to Jim! And that probably explained the fear on Terri's face when she saw him. But how did she know he was a pusher? What had given her a clue? Could it have been Jim and Chester who beat him up that night? All of these questions flashed across Kurt's mind in rapid succession.

"Aren't you afraid of being caught?" the new customer asked.

"No one knows I'm here, except Jim and you," Chester said. "And I don't think you'll be doing any talking because you would be involved."

"He hid in the back seat of my car, and I drove him in ... right in front of the sponsors," Jim said laughing.

By now Kurt recognized the other voice as that of Jesse Thornton. He had been the star quarterback on the football team.

There was no talk now, just some deep sighs, and an occasional "Wow!"

"You okay, Jesse?" Jim asked.

"Sure, I'm ready to face anything now. We should be the life of the party after this. I feel as if I could float right in there."

"Yeah, I know what you mean," Jim said. "I'm seeing stars myself."

A CALL IN THE NIGHT

After Jesse, there were others. Jim would bring them out, and after a short discussion with Chester, Kurt could see the faint glow of another joint being consumed.

Kurt wanted to get back to the lodge where he could either call the police, or alert someone to what was going on, but he couldn't take the chance of being seen. The memory of sharp knuckles striking his face was still fresh in his mind. He knew a lot more about drugs and pushers now than he had six months earlier.

After about an hour, Kurt decided he could wait no longer, so he crept around to the back side of the well-house, and then made a dash for the back door of the lodge. He opened the door as quietly as possible, and checked to see if there was anyone in the back hall.

Everything seemed to be the same at the party as when he and Terri had left. Some kids were playing games, others were eating, and a few were dancing to the music of a small band, and still others were just stretched out in big chairs before the fire. Here and there couples were huddled together, either relaxing in each other's arms, or in deep conversation.

As far as Kurt could tell, no one had missed him for which he was thankful. He wasn't ready to answer any questions . . . at least not yet. He had to decide what to do, and he needed time to think. He could call Sergeant Larson, but it was almost 3:00 a.m., and he knew the Sergeant would not be at the station. Should he talk to someone else? He thought of talking to a sponsor, but he wasn't sure how they would handle the situation.

Finally, he decided to sit down in one of the empty chairs before the fire and collect his thoughts. He stretched out, put his head back, and began to sort out the events of the past two hours. And even though his mind was whirling, he was so totally drained, both emotionally and physically, that he dropped off to sleep immediately.

He was awakened by the sound of a telephone ringing. He quickly looked at his watch. It was 5:30. He had been sleeping for over two hours! Then it all came back to him . . . Terri . . .

Jim . . . Chester . . . and he jumped to his feet.

He stretched to relieve the tension in his back and neck. Apparently he had been in the same position, for the whole two hours. As he did so, he realized he was hungry, and in almost the same moment discovered why. From the kitchen was coming the sweet odor of frying bacon, and he could hear tables being set up for breakfast.

The phone rang several more times before someone answered it. He could hear the voice of one of the adult sponsors who had volunteered to cook breakfast. The voice was quiet and subdued at first, and then began to rise in a quick crescendo as each new word was blurted out. The one thing he could hear over and over was, "Oh no! It can't be! It just can't be!"

By this time, the boys who were playing fussball had heard the voice and had quit playing. Several others who had been quietly talking were up on their feet and running toward the kitchen. It was obvious to everyone that something terrible had happened, and a kind of panic swept over the crowd. Something wrong, but they didn't know what it was.

By the time the telephone conversation was finished, most of the kids had crowded around the kitchen door, peering anxiously inside. When Mrs. Wilson hung up the receiver, she reached for a chair. Her face was ashen and she seemed about to faint.

"What is it, Helen?" her husband asked, as he helped her to a chair.

"It's Jim Hagen," she said weakly. "He missed the curve going back into town, and there's been a terrible accident."

"Is he hurt?" several asked, almost in unison.

"They don't know for sure about Jim, but there were others in the car. One was taken to the hospital, and they can't find the third. The police want us to check who else might have been with Jim."

About that time, Kurt remembered Terri, and began to look around the crowd for her. First his eyes just skimmed the group, and then he started to push kids aside to get a better look.

"Where's Terri?" he asked, almost frantically.

"Oh, no!" Mary Osterberg said, her face turning white. "I remember seeing Terri leave with Jim a couple hours ago."

"Are you sure," Kurt said, grabbing Mary by the arms.

"I'm positive," Mary said. "I remember wondering why at the time because I knew she had come with you."

"If only I had . . . " Kurt gasped, his mind racing over the events of the night.

"Had what?" Cindy asked, stepping up to Kurt's side.

"If only I hadn't fallen asleep," Kurt finally said. "Maybe I could have talked her out of it."

"But who was the third?" Mrs. Wilson asked.

Everyone looked around and tried to guess, but by the process of elimination, they could account for everyone else. "There just isn't anyone else," Kurt said.

"There has to be," Mrs. Wilson said. "The first person at the scene found a third person unconscious, but when they got back from calling the police and an ambulance, there were only two."

"I've got to see Terri," Kurt said, starting toward the door.

"Someone had better go with you," Mr. Wilson said. "In your state of mind, you might have another accident."

"We'll go with him," Cindy said, grabbing Brad's arm.

Kurt didn't answer, but kept walking. Cindy and Brad caught up with him.

"But why would Terri go with him?" Cindy asked as soon as they got in the car. "She came with you, didn't she?"

"It's all my fault," Kurt said, starting the motor.

"Your fault? Why?" she asked.

"We had an argument," Kurt answered.

"And she decided not to go back with you?"

"Guess so," Kurt replied as he turned onto

the main road and pushed the accelerator. "I fell asleep, and when I woke up, she was gone."

"But why Jim?" Brad asked. "Everyone knows what kind of a driver he is . . . and besides he was probably stoned."

"You mean he's on drugs?" Cindy asked.

"Sure, I thought everyone knew that. If you wanted drugs at school, all you had to do was ask Jim. He always knew where to get them."

"That still doesn't explain why Terri went with him," Cindy said.

"I can verify that Jim was stoned," Kurt said.

"You can?" Cindy asked. But before Kurt could answer, Cindy said, "Watch that curve, or we'll miss it like Jim did."

Flashing lights still marked the scene of the accident as they slowed down. Two police cars were on the scene, plus a number of curious people who had stopped. A small crowd was gathered along the edge of the road looking off into the nearby field.

"Should we stop?" Kurt asked.

"According to the call, they're already at the hospital, so why not go directly there?" Cindy answered.

When they got back on the straight road again, Brad said, "You were saying you can verify Jim was using drugs tonight?"

"Yes, and I think I know who the third person

was in the car," Kurt answered.

"Who?" Brad asked.

"Remember that middle-aged man, slightly bald who seems to be around the Hagens' whenever there is a party?" Kurt asked.

"I'll explain later, but I'm sure this Chester, as Jim calls him, was the third person. If he was able to walk at all, he got out of there so the police wouldn't find him."

"Sounds logical," Brad said. "You may have to convince the police that you are right."

"If only I had alerted someone right away instead of going to sleep, they would never have gotten away," Kurt said.

As they drove on, Kurt remembered again how suddenly Terri had wanted to leave Jim's party when she saw Chester. Why was she in the car with him now? There was obviously still a lot about her that he didn't know. As they pulled into the hospital parking lot, Kurt knew he needed to talk to her again . . . now more than ever before.

THE WAIT

The three went into the waiting room. Since it was so early, no one else was there. A receptionist came to the window which separated the waiting room from the business office.

"May I help you?" the woman said. Her voice was as colorless as the white walls around her.

"There was an accident, and we were told the victims were brought here," Kurt said.

"Are you family?" the attendant asked.

"No . . . just friends," Kurt answered.

"Visiting hours begin at 9:00 a.m.," she said.

"But we have to know how they are," Kurt said, almost pleading.

"What are their names?"

"Jim Hagen and Terri Turner."

"Wait here," she said in a crisp, commanding voice.

The receptionist went to her desk and dialed a number. After some low conversation which the three could not hear, she put one hand over the mouthpiece and turned to them. "What are your names?" she asked.

"I'm Kurt Lang, and I'm especially interested in knowing about Terri Turner," he answered.

The attendant relayed the message, and there was some more discussion before she came to the window.

"If you'll just have a seat, someone from the family will be here to see you," she said.

"Can't you just tell us how they are?" Kurt said.

"I'm sorry, I can't do that." And with that she turned back to her desk.

Cindy, Brad and Kurt found three chairs near each other and sat in silence, waiting.

After about ten minutes, Kurt said, "I'd better phone my dad so he knows what has happened. He'll be expecting me home soon."

"We should do the same," Cindy said, and Brad nodded.

Kurt went to a pay phone at the end of the waiting room and called his dad. After explaining the situation, his dad was satisfied, and asked him to call back as soon as he knew anything more.

142

Kurt sat down again and Cindy and Brad made their calls. When Brad came back, he said, "My folks are waiting for me to come home so we can go to my uncle's for the weekend."

"Why don't you go on?" Cindy said. "I'll stay here with Kurt."

"Sure you don't mind?" Brad asked.

"No. Go ahead. Kurt can take me home later. You didn't know Terri as well as we did, anyway."

As Brad started to leave, he turned around, "I can't. We took the bus to the party, and I came with you to the hospital, so I don't have a car."

"Here," Kurt said, getting out his keys. "Use mine. Cindy and I will get home some way. If nothing else, Dad will come to get us."

"Thanks a lot. I'll leave it out in front of the house so you can pick it up later. Where shall I leave the keys?"

"Just put them under the mat," Kurt said.

So Brad left, and Cindy and Kurt sat down again. After a few minutes of silence, Cindy reached over and placed her hand over Kurt's and said, "Kurt, I'm sorry. Really I am."

"Thanks, Cindy," Kurt said. "You're a real friend." And then he turned his hand over so that their fingers became entwined.

After what seemed like an eternity, they heard steps coming down the hall toward the waiting room, and Jan came around the corner. Her eyes were red, and it was obvious she had been crying. Kurt and Cindy stood up, and Jan came with her arms outstretched. They stood in the middle of the waiting room floor with their arms around each other like football players in a huddle.

No one spoke, but Jan began to sob on Kurt's shoulder, and Kurt and Cindy began to cry, too.

Jan motioned for them to sit down, and she sat between them, holding one by each hand.

"How is she?" Kurt finally asked the question which was uppermost on his mind.

"I'm afraid she's gone," Jan said.

"You mean she . . . she's dead?" Cindy gasped.

Jan nodded her head.

Kurt sank back in his chair and put his hands over his face. For the second time that night hot tears began to flow from between his fingers. "Oh, no," is all he could say.

After Cindy and Kurt composed themselves somewhat, Jan said, "She probably died instantly, but they thought they felt some pulse, so they brought her here, but she was pronounced dead on arrival."

Then turning to Kurt, she said, "If she had only stayed with you, it wouldn't have happened."

"I know, " Kurt said. "It's all my fault. I killed her . . . I killed her."

"Don't say that," Jan said, taking his hand. "She didn't have to go with Jim, did she?"

"No, even if she didn't want to go back with me, she could have taken the school bus," Kurt said. "But it's still my fault."

"What happened between you two tonight?" Cindy asked.

Kurt took a deep breath. He didn't know how much he should tell, and how much should remain his secret. He merely said they had gone for a walk, and had had an argument. "If I had been more sensitive to her feelings, it never would have happened. I tried to show her that I loved her, but apparently I didn't know how. I failed at love just like I've failed at everything else."

"I think there are some things about Terri you don't know," Jan said. "I had hoped you would never need to know, but I think now it would be best if you did.

"Terri's home life was very bad," she began.

"That she told me," Kurt said.

"But I'm not sure she told you that she was hooked on drugs by the time she was in junior high. She'd get so spaced out they would find her passed out on the lavatory floor at school."

"Terri?" they said almost in unison.

"I know. She could put up quite a front. At times she seemed so loving, so innocent. It was hard for people to believe that such a beautiful person could be hooked on drugs. Someone introduced her to them at a very early age. I've always suspected it was her father."

"But she wasn't that way here," Cindy said. "I knew her well, and I never saw her high on drugs, or even heard her talk about it."

"Again, I say, she was a great actress. She was finally put in a de-tox center last year, and took the cure, but just to be sure, she came up here to live with me. It took her away from the old crowd and introduced her to a whole new set of friends—like you two. I was hoping she would find Christ through the church and kids her own age—like you, but I guess it didn't work. Relatives are always the hardest people in the world to witness to."

"Think of the opportunities I missed to talk to her about Christ," Kurt said. "Like last week after the party. I really blew it then. She wanted to talk about the speaker's message, but I kept getting her off the subject. He really got her to thinking."

"Did she stay off drugs here?" Cindy asked.

"I'm not sure," Jan said. "Certainly she was a lot better, but lately, I've been worried. There have been some calls that made me suspicious. She was with Jim Hagen a number of times, and it's assumed he has drug ties. I can't help but believe that her ride tonight had something to do with drugs."

"I know Jim had been smoking pot tonight," Kurt said, "because I saw him."

Kurt related what he had seen in the parking lot and how he had planned to call the police, but fell asleep instead.

"So, you see, I can prove that Jim was high on drugs when Terri was killed," Kurt said.

"I hope so," Jan answered, "but the Hagens have plenty of money, and they've been able to get Jim off the hook before by just hiring a good lawyer. If you're willing to testify, be ready for a lot of hassle."

"But he killed Terri, and I'll do anything I can to get him convicted," Kurt said.

"The only thing that still isn't clear in my mind is why she would have started into town with Jim," Jan said. "If she wanted drugs, Jim had them right there."

"Jim is the only one who could answer that—if he would," Kurt said. "Of course, there is always Chester, but who knows where he is."

"Chester?" Jan asked.

"There was a third person in the car," Kurt said, "and he was the pusher I was talking about."

Just then Jim's parents came into the waiting room. They, too, looked tired, and as if they had been crying.

"How's Jim?" Jan asked.

"He'll be all right," his mother said. "They just

took him to surgery to set his broken leg, but when they get a cast on it, he should be up and around—maybe out of here in a couple of days."

"We're sorry to hear about Terri," Mr. Hagen said, reaching out his hand to Jan.

"What really happened?" Jan asked as she accepted his hand. "What did Jim tell you?"

"I don't think we should discuss it," Mr. Hagen said. "I'm sure it will all come out in an investigation. I understand one has already been started."

The way Mr. Hagen talked, he seemed so cold, so indifferent that Kurt wanted to cry out, "Don't you realize Jim killed someone—someone I loved very much?"

But he didn't.

ANOTHER HOSPITAL VISIT

Kurt and Cindy stayed with Jan until she had made the necessary arrangements with the hospital, and then Jan took them by Brad's house so that Kurt could get his car. They offered to stay with Jan, but she said she needed to be alone for a little while. She needed time to think through the funeral arrangements, and to call Terri's parents.

Kurt dropped Cindy off in front of her house, and then turned into his own drive. As Cindy left the car, Kurt said, "Thanks for staying with me. I guess I needed someone more than I thought."

"That's what friends are for," Cindy said.

"It's nice to have a neighbor who is also a friend," Kurt answered, managing a smile.

Kurt's dad was eating breakfast as he walked into his house, so the two of them sat around the kitchen table for awhile talking. His dad offered to make Kurt something to eat, but Kurt's stomach was in such a turmoil he knew he wouldn't be able to keep anything down if he tried to eat. He explained to his dad, as best he could, the details of the accident.

"Ironic, isn't it?" his dad said. "I lost the only one I ever loved, and now you have lost your first love."

"You really loved Mom, didn't you?" Kurt asked.

"She was everything to me. In fact she was the first girl I fell in love with, and by the time I was your age, I had already made wedding plans. I loved her so much that no one could ever take her place.

"Is that why you never re-married?" Kurt asked.

"I know now that I was selfish, and it wasn't fair to make you grow up without a mother, but I just couldn't open my heart to anyone else. The trouble is that I closed my heart to just about everyone after she died. I . . . well, I'm not sure how to say it, but I'm afraid I even closed it to you."

Kurt had never seen his father in this mood. It was the first time they had ever discussed his mother's death.

"Don't be so hard on yourself, Dad," Kurt said. "You've been a good father. You've given me everything I needed and more."

His father got up and came around the table, putting his arms around Kurt from the back. "I'm not sure I gave you the one thing you needed most—love. Son, I'm sorry about Terri, and I want you to know that I do understand your heartache."

Kurt got up, and the two of them held each other tightly for a long time. It was as if they were both afraid if they broke the spell, it would be gone forever.

"Dad, I love you," Kurt said for the first time since he was a little boy. "Thanks for being my dad."

By this time tears were running down his dad's face, and when they finally let go of each other, he said, "Son, maybe you don't believe it, but I love you, too."

Kurt was so choked up that he couldn't talk any more, so he went to his room and laid down on the bed. His mind was in a turmoil. He kept dozing, but each time he did, he woke up in the middle of a nightmare.

Finally he sat up in bed and tried to convince himself that everything that had happened had been part of one bad nightmare, but then he realized again it was for real.

About 3:00 that afternoon he showered,

shaved, and put on a robe. He was hungry, so he went to the kitchen and heated some soup. As he sat by the kitchen table, he rehearsed over and over in his mind the events of the previous night. Everything seemed to fall into place except why Terri had gone with Jim ... and only Jim knew the answer to that question. By the time he had finished his soup, he decided he should pay Jim a visit.

Once again, Kurt entered the hospital and asked at the desk for Jim Hagen's room. He was glad this was another shift, and a new attendant was on duty. "Room 435," he was told, so he headed for the elevators. He got out on the fourth floor, and followed the signs to 435. As he approached the room, he wondered what he was going to say. It was hard to feel sorry for Jim because of what he had seen that evening. And Kurt still remembered Jim's threats and suspected he was involved in the beating he had taken.

As he came to the door, he looked in to see who was there. Kurt had not made too many hospital calls, so he wasn't sure just what to expect. Fortunately, Jim was alone in the room. He was lying back on his bed with one leg slightly elevated and in a cast.

"Hi, Jim," Kurt said, entering the room.

"Well, I didn't expect to see you!" Jim said, looking uncomfortable at Kurt's presence.

"How's it going?" Kurt asked, for want of something better to say.

"My leg will be okay," Jim said, turning his face to the window, "but they tell me Terri didn't make it."

"That's what I wanted to talk to you about," Kurt said.

"I suspected that," Jim said. "I didn't force her to go with me, if that's what you want to know."

"But why did she go? There must have been a reason," Kurt said.

"You know why she didn't want to go with you, I don't," Jim said.

"I know that, but I'm asking why, of all people, she went back with you?"

"She asked to."

"But why?" Kurt insisted.

"Maybe I had something she wanted," Jim said.

"Drugs?" Kurt asked.

"I didn't say that," Jim said. "You did."

"Don't beat around the bush," Kurt replied. "I know you'd been smoking pot. You were probably too high to see the road."

"You've got to be kidding," Jim laughed nervously. "How could I get pot at a school-sponsored party?"

"You don't need to lie to me," Kurt said, stepping closer to the bed. "I happened to be watching when Chester gave it to you ... and I saw you smoke it. I even saw you bring others out to buy from Chester."

"Were you alone?" Jim asked. "Anybody with you?"

"Why?"

"If there wasn't, then it's your word against mine, and I'm saying there was no Chester, no pot, and that you're lying."

"What about the person who said there were three in the car at the accident?" Kurt said.

"Did they find anyone else?"

"No, somehow your pusher managed to escape between the time people found you and the time the police arrived."

"You think you know an awful lot," Jim sneered, his face beginning to flush.

"I know enough to say that you and your pot killed Terri," Kurt said, feeling his temper beginning to rise.

"Your little Terri wasn't as sweet and innocent as you thought. You were so naive you didn't know what was going on. She was on drugs all the time. In fact, we ... I mean, I didn't have anything strong enough for her last night. We were going for some coke when I missed the curve. Now you know, but I'll deny I ever said it. And you'd better keep your mouth shut about all of this. You know what happened to you the last time!"

"So, it was you," Kurt said.

"Yes, and I'll do it again if I get a chance."

"Who was the other one, Chester?"

"You better get out of here," Jim said. "I just came out of surgery a few hours ago, and I'm still a sick man."

"Not half as sick as you would be if I could get my hands on you," Kurt said.

"Now who is threatening whom?" Jim said, sneering. "I thought Christians turned the other cheek!"

His words stung Kurt, and he just stood and glared at Jim.

"You get out of here, or I'll call a nurse and have you thrown out." Jim tried to sit up in bed.

"I'll leave, but you had better think up some good excuses because I'm going to the police with everything I know."

Kurt turned to leave.

"We have ways of stopping people like you from talking. Maybe the next time it will be more permanent," Jim called after him.

As he continued toward the door, Jim called again, "Just remember, you could make it a lot easier on yourself and everyone else if you forget everything we talked about today. You'll never be able to prove it, and the only one who could testify is dead."

"And you killed her!" Kurt shot back. "But

155

you're wrong, there is one more ... if we can find him."

"He's too professional," Jim said. "He'll never be caught."

Hot tears were streaming down his face as Kurt half-ran down the hall. He was emotionally drained ... and angry. He knew what had happened. Now his job would be to convince the police that he was right.

THE FUNERAL

Terri had been so badly disfigured in the accident that there was no reviewal time scheduled at the funeral home. Kurt was glad because he wasn't sure he could handle seeing Terri in a casket. A memorial service was planned for Monday morning at 10:00, after which time Jan would fly back to Dallas with the body for another family funeral and burial.

Kurt had not been to a funeral since his mother's, and since he had been only eight at the time, he couldn't remember much about it. He did remember the sadness that had come over him when he saw his father cry, and the lonely feeling he had when he and his father were home alone for the first time. He remembered how long it was before his dad would laugh and play with him again.

Now Kurt was faced with another funeral—one he wished he could avoid. Cindy tried to make it as easy as possible for him. She seemed to sense how deeply he was hurting more than anyone else. His dad had to be out of town on business that Monday, so he couldn't go to the funeral. When Cindy heard about it, she invited Kurt to go with her and her family.

Kurt liked both Cindy's dad and mother, but he was especially fond of her mother. She had been a second mother to him after his own had died. She always thought of including Kurt when she took her own children any place. Kurt had come to love and respect her. She had been responsible for taking him to Sunday School and church, and he had sensed, even as a child, that the one thing she wanted more than anything else was for him to become a Christian. She had been delighted when Kurt had told her of his decision in his Sunday School class that morning.

So when the funeral began in the chapel, Kurt was seated with Cindy's family next to Cindy. He had assumed their pastor would have the funeral, but was surprised when the Minister of Youth came out from behind the screen.

It seemed so incongruous to Kurt to hear someone that young talk about death, and the thought of a seventeen-year-old girl's body in the casket seemed even more out of place.

Funerals had always been for adults—usually old people. At least that's what he'd thought.

And Kurt was equally surprised to see how many young people were in the audience. It seemed the whole youth group from church was there, plus some of Terri's friends from high school. There were a number from the senior class, and even some from other classes who had ridden the bus with her.

So it was a young preacher, talking to a young audience about the death of a young person—all quite different from Kurt's stereotype of a funeral. In fact, the whole funeral was different. The preacher had the congregation sing a hymn, and then a member of the youth group pulled up a stool before a mike and sang several contemporary numbers, accompanying himself on the guitar. He sang haunting melodies about life and death, but none of them were somber. Some of them were almost humorous.

"How can they treat this tragedy so lightly?" Kurt thought. The hurt in his heart simply did not match the assurance which the songs portrayed. He wondered if they were insensitive, or if he had become too emotionally involved with Terri and the accident to put death in its proper perspective.

The pastor read some passages from the Bible about heaven, and made it sound as if death were merely going home. He made it sound like a warm, loving place—even more of a home than he had ever known on earth.

Then the pastor began to talk directly to the audience, especially the young people in it.

"The illustration we have before us today of the brevity of life should cause each of us to re-evaluate our own lives. If Terri could talk to us today, knowing what she now knows, I think she would say, 'Prepare for eternity before it is too late. Live life to its fullest, but always with eternity in mind.'

"In a sense, Terri was a stranger in our midst. She came unknown, and she left us only partly known. Some of us may have tried to get to know her, but most of us went our own way, did our own things, spent time with our own friends, and never went out of our way to make her feel a part of us. The tragedy of her death is that none of us are really sure where she stood in her relationship to God. Her sudden death should remind all of us that we need to make use of every opportunity we have to tell someone about Christ. We may have only one opportunity to do so. We can't blow that opportunity when it comes our way."

Kurt cringed at the pastor's words. He remembered how much Terri had wanted to talk about spiritual things after the church graduation banquet, and how he had deliberately steered the conversation in another direction.

"And what about you?" the pastor continued. "If your life should suddenly end tonight, would you be prepared to meet God? It isn't the length of life that counts, it is what you have done with the years He has given to you. They can be lived for self and wasted, or they can be lived for Christ and count for eternity.

"Christ wants you to respond to His invitation today. If you do not know Christ as Savior, He stands ready to make you His child. And if you are a Christian and have not been living for Christ, He waits to give purpose to your life. He wants to make something beautiful out of it. He isn't asking you to clean up your life first, just turn it over to Him and let Him do the cleaning.

"I'm going to ask you to do something I've never done at any funeral before," the preacher said. "I'm going to ask those who would like to make a public commitment to Christ, either for salvation or for dedication, to come up here and stand with me around Terri's casket. If you want to say, 'Lord, forgive me. Take me and make the most out of my life—regardless of whether I die tomorrow or in old age—come up here and stand with me and we will have prayer together. Let us pray."

Kurt bowed his head. His heart and mind churned with a mixture of emotions. He was grieving over the loss of Terri, but now he was also deeply convicted that he had not done what he could to bring her to Christ. If anything, he had done the opposite, he had led her away from Christ.

He tried to pray, but words simply would not come. He was no longer conscious of anyone else in the room except God and him. Then, almost as if he were watching from the outside, he saw himself get up from his chair, push past others in the row, and go up the aisle toward the casket. Tears began to fill his eyes, so that the pastor and the casket became blurred, but as he reached the front, he felt the warm hand of the pastor's in his own, and a strong arm around his shoulder.

Kurt wasn't alone for long. In a moment, he felt someone else by his side. A familiar hand reached out and took his, and he squeezed it to recognize Cindy's presence. Then from everywhere in the audience, other kids came, crowding around the casket. Some were weeping openly, and others were quietly praying.

Kurt's prayer that day was simple, direct, and life-changing. He said, "Lord, you know me better than I know myself. You know how I have failed in the past, and I ask you to forgive me. You know how many years I have left on earth. If you can use these years to your glory, here I am, take me."

After almost every young person in the audience was standing around the casket, the pastor prayed. He asked God to make the decisions which had been made that day real to each one. Then he pronounced the benediction and dismissed the crowd.

Both Jan and Cindy's mother came up immediately and hugged Kurt and Cindy. There were few words, but more crying, and Kurt left that day feeling more loved than he had ever felt in his life.

There was a lunch at the church before Terri's body was to be moved to the airport for its trip to Dallas, but Kurt didn't feel like talking to anyone, so he and Cindy took her mother to the church, and then went back to her house.

"Want to come in for a little while?" Cindy asked.

"I have an appointment with Sergeant Larson at the police station at 1:00 p.m., but I could come in until then," Kurt answered.

"Good," Cindy said. "I'll make us some lunch."

They went to the kitchen, and Kurt took a chair and watched Cindy as she took some hamburger out of the refrigerator, made it into patties, and put them into the electric skillet.

As he watched her, he realized how long it had been since he had really looked at her. Her light brown hair looked especially soft in the sunlight streaming through the kitchen window.

She was wearing a white blouse and blue skirt. Kurt remembered they were the clothes she had worn on Friday night for graduation.

"Did you suspect that Terri had a drug problem?" she asked, without looking up from her work.

"Never. I did wonder why she had come up here during her senior year, but when she told us about her parents separating, I just assumed that was the main reason. How could I have been so blind? I thought I had learned a lot about drugs doing that story, but I obviously needed to learn a lot more."

"I'm afraid Christians are blind to a lot of problems in our world. I did make an effort to become her friend, but if I had understood her problem better, I could have been of more help," Cindy said.

"But why did it have to turn out this way?" Kurt asked, as much to himself as to Cindy.

"Who knows?" Cindy answered. "But there must be a reason."

"If I could see a reason, it would help a lot," Kurt said.

"Maybe we've seen one reason today," Cindy said beginning to set the table.

"Yeah. I suppose God used her death to teach us ... especially me ... a lesson. But couldn't He have made the lesson less painful?"

"You really cared about her, didn't you?"

Cindy asked as she sat down across from Kurt.

"I loved her from the first moment I saw her, but I was never really able to convince her of it," Kurt said.

"It seems to me you did everything you could," Cindy said. "You can't love someone who doesn't want to be loved."

"They say love is blind, and maybe it is. I still loved her even though I suspected she was the one who tipped off Jim and his pusher where I was that night."

"How do you know it was Jim?" Cindy asked.

"He told me."

"And you still cared about her?"

"Yeah. Dumb, isn't it?" Kurt said.

"Either that or a great illustration of the love of God," Cindy answered.

"Right now it just sounds dumb;" Kurt said.

"What happened in that cabin?"

He dropped his eyes from hers. He knew what she was thinking, and it hurt.

"Nothing. Really," Kurt said.

"Nothing? Then why did she get so upset?" Cindy asked.

"It's hard to explain, but because nothing happened, everything happened."

"That's double talk. You'll have to explain."

"I wanted something to happen very much. I arranged everything, but when we got alone, it was entirely different than I had anticipated. I thought she was waiting for me to prove my love through sex, but she said that was all wrong—that love was something beyond the physical. Apparently she had experienced plenty of sex, and now she wanted something deeper ... something I didn't know how to give her."

"But love is a two way street," Cindy responded. "It has to be received as well as given, and I can't see that she did much about receiving it."

"But I realize now that I didn't know much about love. I'm just beginning to learn. I even told my dad I loved him for the first time in years. Well, going back to that night . . . we argued about the differences between love and sex, and she left, unhappy and disappointed with me. She said she expected more from a Christian. The last words I ever heard her say were, 'I love you too much to say yes.' I'll hear that the rest of my life."

"At least she kept you from doing something wrong," Cindy said. "You should be thankful for that."

"But, you see, it was because of the argument that she apparently decided to get stoned. She went to Jim for some coke . . . he told me that. When he didn't have any, they started into town for it."

"You can't blame yourself for her death. She made her own decision to go with Jim," Cindy said, trying to comfort Kurt.

"But it all started with my decision to take that key," he said sadly.

Shadows dimmed Cindy's eyes as she answered, "Yes. And that's a decision you will have to learn to live with."

AT THE POLICE STATION

Kurt was somewhat apprehensive about his visit to the police station. He understood now the consequences of involvement in drug control. When he had done his school story, he had gone into it with little thought or fear for the consequences. But now he knew how vicious drugs could be, and how ruthless drug pushers could be to those who got in their way.

So he went to the police knowing full well that his life might be in danger if he told them everything he knew. But he was determined to do so. Life wasn't as important to him now as it had been a few months ago. He prayed as he drove to the station that God would give him the words to say, and the courage to do what was right...regardless of what it might mean to him. He told God he was ready to die for Him if necessary. Later, he thought back upon that day and wondered how he would have reacted if God had taken him up on that prayer; but for that day, he was as honest with God as he knew how to be.

When he got to the station, he was ushered into a small room with a table and a few chairs. Sergeant Larson and another policeman came in and sat down across from him. One had a pad and pencil to take notes. First they read him his rights, and asked him if he understood that anything he might say could be used in a court of law, and that he might be forced to testify publicly about the things he would say.

He said he understood.

Sergeant Larson chatted with him a little about his first visit. Then Larson said, "How well did you know Terri Turner?"

"Quite well. We had been dating for six months."

"Did she go with you to the graduation party?"

"Yes."

"Did you expect her to return with you?"

"Yes."

"Why didn't she?"

"We had an argument, and she decided to go home with Jim Hagen."

"An argument? Over what?"

Kurt waited. He looked across the table and saw four eyes piercing him. "Over the meaning of love," he finally answered.

"Explain that," Larson said, while the other man took notes.

"Over whether love had to be physical to be love."

"You mean you were arguing over whether or not to have sex?"

Kurt winced at the bluntness of the question. "Yeah, you can say that," he answered.

"And did you?"

"No."

"Where did this argument take place?"

"In one of the cabins."

"And what did she do after the argument?"

"She left me, and apparently went back to the lodge."

"And what did you do?"

"I waited a little while, and then I, too, started back to the lodge."

"And you were telling me on the phone you saw something peculiar on the way back," Larson said.

"Yeah. On the way back I saw Jim Hagen and an older man...a man he calls Chester...in the

171

parking lot smoking pot. Then I watched as Jim brought a number of the kids from the party out to the lot for a smoke."

"Could you identify this Chester if you saw him?"

"Certainly."

"Why? Had you seen him before?"

"He was at that party which you raided at the Hagens' last fall," Kurt said.

The two men talked to each other, and then went into an adjoining office. "We'll be back with something to show you," Larson said.

Soon they came back with several pictures. "Can you identify the individual you call Chester from these pictures?" he asked.

Kurt looked over the half-dozen pictures before him, then pointing to one he said, "This is Chester . . . yeah, that's him."

"You're sure?"

"Positive."

"Would you be willing to tell that in a court of law?"

"Yes," Kurt replied, once again realizing the consequences of what he was saying.

"Would you have any idea where this Chester might be?"

"No," Kurt said, "but I know he spends a lot of time at the Hagens'. He's been there both times I've been there, and others have seen him there. It shouldn't be difficult to identify him if you can find him soon because he should still have some injuries from the accident."

"The first call that came to us mentioned three individuals hurt, but when our men got there they only found two. If we find him, and he does have some injuries, it would certainly prove your theory. The sooner we find him the better."

"Could I ask you something?" Kurt said. "How is it that you have a picture of Chester?"

"Chester is an assumed name. The man you identified as Chester is really Bernie Adams, a known drug pusher from Dallas, Texas. We had a tip he was operating in this area. In fact, we had a tip he was at Hagens' the night of the raid, but we didn't find him there."

"Do you remember whether it was a man's or a woman's voice on the phone that night when you received the tip?" Kurt asked, suddenly anxious.

"I took the call," the other officer said, "and if I remember correctly it sounded like a young girl. Why?"

"You know Terri was from Dallas, and when she saw him at the party that night, she panicked, and made us leave. But why would she turn him in if she was on drugs herself?"

"The drug business is a strange business,"

173

Larson said. "Maybe she had an old score to settle with him. Maybe he was her pusher in Dallas. Who knows?"

"Everything you have said seems to fit together," the other officer said, "but what proof do you think you can give us that it is true? I'm sure you realize Jim Hagen has told us quite another story."

"I guess you will just have to decide who to believe. Unless . . . unless I still have something," Kurt said, feeling in his jacket pocket.

As he reached into the pocket, his fingers closed once again around the familiar key. "Here, this should prove my story about being in the cabin. I still have the key, and there is no other way it would be in my pocket. In fact, if you check out the cabin, you will probably find it just as I left it with the door unlocked, and the davenport uncovered."

The officer took the key for evidence. It was clearly marked, "Idahope—Nurse's Cabin."

An all-points bulletin was put out for Chester . . . or Bernie's . . . arrest, and a few days later, Kurt received a call from the police station asking him to come down again for questioning. When he arrived, he was taken into a line-up room where six men were standing with their backs against the wall.

"Can you identify the man you call Chester

from among these men?" Sergeant Larson asked.

Kurt scanned the line-up and without hesitation pointed out the one he had seen both at the Hagens' and in the parking lot.

And he had a deep, fresh scar on his forehead.

That night Kurt slept without fear for the first time since the accident.

A NEW LOVE

Kurt went back to work at the clothing store. His father had found a lawyer to help him prepare for the upcoming trial, and had advised Kurt to stay around town to be available for questioning. If this had not been necessary, he probably would have gone with Cindy to be a counselor at their church camp that summer.

As it was, he found himself alone much of the time, and extremely lonely. He enjoyed being with the kids from the church, but most of the youth activities had been suspended for the summer months, and a lot of the kids were gone on vacation.

About the only one who was around town

most of the summer was Brad, and they frequently did things together. One Saturday afternoon Brad called to see if Kurt wanted to go swimming at the lake. It was a beautiful day, and neither of them had to work.

They swam for a little while, and then went up on the beach and laid down on the warm sand. They were silent at first, and then Brad said, "You're going to have to get over Terri sooner or later."

"I've accepted what happened," Kurt answered.

"But you haven't been the same since the accident," Brad said. "You're no fun to be around anymore. You can't go on grieving for her the rest of your life."

"It's not so much grief as it is disappointment. And I'm still disappointed with myself. To think she misled me as she did. I keep thinking I could have helped her, but I didn't. I could have been an influence on her instead of letting her influence me the way she did."

"You still blame yourself for the accident, don't you?" Brad asked.

"I can't help it," Kurt answered. "I did care about her, and even though she wasn't what she appeared to be, I still miss her. It's especially bad right now because I can't run next door to the Johnstons' and talk to Cindy. She's been a great help."

178

"You like Cindy a lot, don't you?" Brad said.

"Sure. I've always liked her," Kurt answered. "She's been like a sister to me."

"Nothing more than a sister?"

"We've been through all of this before," Kurt answered shortly. "Anyway, she's your girl, and I don't mess around with other guy's girls— especially when they're bigger than me." Kurt laughed and threw a handful of sand at Brad.

Brad got to his knees and began scooping sand on Kurt.

"See what I mean?" Kurt said. "I don't have a chance with bullies like you."

"Just to prove what a friend I am," Brad said, "I'm going to tell you that Cindy isn't my girl."

"But you've been dating her most of the year."

"I know, but our relationship isn't going anywhere. It's a friendship—firm, solid—but only a friendship."

"So what do you want me to do about it?"

"If you don't know by now, I'm not going to tell you. Cindy is coming home next weekend, and I suggest you do a little work on your own. After all, you're a graduate now."

Kurt winced—he had heard that term before. He had been through a short course in life the last few weeks, but he wasn't sure he had graduated.

That night Kurt spent some time thinking about his conversation with Brad. "Could it be," he asked himself, "that I have really been in love with Cindy all of these years and didn't realize it? If so, what about her?" Terri had told Kurt how much Cindy thought of him, but he hadn't believed her.

He remembered how warm and loving she had been to him in the hospital, and after the funeral. She had even said she was going to miss him when she left for the summer.

By Friday night, Kurt had decided he would find out for sure if there was anything between him and Cindy before the weekend was over.

He saw the car drop Cindy off late on Friday night, so he waited until he thought she might be awake before he called on Saturday morning.

Mrs. Johnston answered the phone.

"Hi, this is Kurt. Is Cindy up yet?"

"She hasn't been down to breakfast, but I think I hear her up in her room," Mrs. Johnston said.

"Could you have her call me when she comes down?" Kurt asked.

"Just hold on. I'll see if she wants to talk to you now," her mother said.

When she came back to the phone, she said, "Hang on a minute. Cindy will be right down."

Kurt waited.

"Good morning, neighbor. What a pleasant surprise!" Cindy said.

"Wow, you sound happy for this hour on Saturday morning," he said.

"Why shouldn't I be?" Cindy answered. "I've just had the greatest three weeks in my life, and now I'm home for a day and away from the little monsters . . . and besides that, you called."

"You sure have a way of making a fellow feel wanted," Kurt said. "What do you have planned for the day?"

"Haven't talked to the folks yet to see if they have something planned, but I need to go downtown and buy a few things to take back to camp with me. Why?"

"Cindy, I'd like to talk," Kurt said.

"Hmmm . . . sounds interesting. But I thought that's what we are doing."

"Be serious," Kurt said. "I mean talk—talk."

"I'd love to," Cindy answered.

"How about letting me take you shopping," Kurt said. "I have the day off."

"I'll check with the folks and call you right back," Cindy answered.

"Okay, I'll be waiting."

In a few minutes, Cindy called back to say

she was free for the day, and would love to go with Kurt. "I'll be ready about 11:00. Okay?"

"I'll be there," Kurt answered. Kurt picked her up promptly at 11:00 and they went downtown, parked in a ramp, and Kurt began to follow Cindy through a number of stores. After the sixth store, he said, "Hey, I'm hungry. All this walking is hard on a growing boy!"

So they found a little restaurant which they both knew, and got a booth near the back.

After they had ordered, Cindy said, "So, I'm waiting."

"For what?"

"You said you wanted to talk. Are you still trying to find a reason for Terri's death?"

"No," Kurt answered. "I think I have finally resolved that. I still don't know the reason, only God knows that, but a lot of things have happened in my life and the life of the kids at church because of her death. Maybe God did use her to minister to a lot of us. But I don't suppose I will ever forgive myself for not trying to win her to Christ."

"That's hard for me to accept, too. But even if we'd been more faithful in witnessing, we have no guarantee that she would have accepted Him," Cindy answered.

"That's not what I wanted to talk about, though" Kurt said. "I want to talk about us."

"What about us?" Cindy asked, looking

intently into Kurt's face.

"I've been thinking how great you've been to me, and how long we've known each other, and . . ."

"How in spite of it we're still friends?" Cindy laughed.

"Yeah, something like that. I was wondering if there might not be something more than friendship here."

"Are you ready for more?" Cindy asked.

"What do you mean?"

"I knew you would have to get over losing Terri before you could ever care for anyone else."

"Could you care for me?" Kurt asked.

"Before I answer, you tell me. Do you care about me, or am I still just your sister?"

"Cindy," he said, reaching for her hands across the table. "I still don't know much about love, but I know a lot more than I did, and I do care about you deeply. Maybe I've always loved you and didn't know it."

Cindy's eyes began to get moist. "Do you realize how long I have waited to hear you say that?"

"Really?" Kurt said, surprised. "What about Brad?"

"Oh, he's just a good friend. We've talked about it, and he knows how I feel about you."

"So that's what he meant last Saturday," Kurt said.

"What did he say?"

"Never mind," Kurt answered.

Kurt paid the check and they went back to shopping, but this time they were hand in hand, and shopping was no longer a duty to Kurt. He was loving every minute of it.

On the way home they stopped by the lake park, and got out. Kurt was like someone who had just been released from a long prison sentence. He laughed, took off his shoes and ran on the beach. He even chased Cindy around the trees. Finally they collapsed on the sand in each other's arms. Then they sat side by side looking out over the water.

"You know," Kurt said, "I think this is the happiest day of my life."

"Mine, too," Cindy said. "What an unexpected weekend!"

"There's so much more we need to talk about. I don't even know what you plan to do this fall," Kurt said.

"All I know," Cindy answered, "is that I hope any of your future plans include me. In three more weeks I'll be home from camp, and then we can talk more about it."

"Can't wait," Kurt said. "There's so much to do ... so much time to make up." Kurt sounded like a little boy.

"A lot has happened since graduation weekend," Cindy said thoughtfully.

"I graduated academically that weekend. But now I feel like I've graduated spiritually and emotionally."

"One never really graduates in either of those areas," Cindy said. "Maybe we should call it a commencement."

"Thanks for being one of my teachers," Kurt said, drawing her closer to himself.

ANOTHER REASON

The next day Cindy and Kurt went to church together, and Kurt was in a great mood. The choir never sounded better, and he listened through the whole sermon for the first time in years.

"Well, you two look happy today," Jan Holmgren said as she met them on the steps following the service.

"Does it show that much?" Cindy asked.

"I would say that you have either just inherited a million dollars, or you're in love," Jan laughed.

"Forget the million," Kurt said, "we've got something better."

"Say, how about you two having dinner with

me?" Jan asked. "I was just planning to eat somewhere alone, and I would love to have company. I got spoiled when Terri was with me, and now I find myself getting lonely much quicker."

After checking on their parents' plans, they agreed to go with Jan. Kurt followed her to her house, and left his car there, then Jan took them to a restaurant located on the edge of a golf course which served a Sunday buffet. They were able to get a window seat where there was a full view of the wide expanse of green grass, brilliantly lighted by the July sun.

Jan asked about Cindy's camp, and about Kurt's work, but eventually, the subject came back to the one thing which was still on all of their minds—Terri.

"I've wondered about the obituary which appeared in the paper," Kurt said. "Was it right?"

"I guess I don't know what you mean," Jan said.

"Here," Kurt said, taking out his billfold, and removing a neatly folded clipping. "I've been carrying this, waiting for a chance to ask you." He unfolded the clipping. "It says here that Terri was born in Twin Falls. Is that true?"

"Let me see that," Jan said, her face blanching. She took the clipping from Kurt, and studied it for a minute.

"What paper was this in?" Jan asked.

"Some Dallas paper," Kurt answered. "A friend of mine found it and sent it to me."

Jan quietly folded the clipping and handed it back to Kurt. "I suppose there's no harm in you knowing now," she said.

"Knowing what?" he asked.

"Yes, she was born here in Twin Falls ... and I was her mother," Jan said.

"Her mother!" Kurt and Cindy exclaimed in unison.

"Remember, I told you about my soldier boy?" Jan asked.

Kurt nodded.

"When he went to Viet Nam, I was pregnant, but I never told him. I lived with his parents at the time, and when Terri was born, and it looked as if we wouldn't be married, they suggested that I put her up for adoption. I was only 17 at the time, and they thought I was much too young to raise her properly. Well, my sister had been married for several years—she's three years older than me—and had found she couldn't have any children. She offered to adopt Terri, so I gave her up when she was just two months old."

"Terri told us she didn't know when she was born—that her mother celebrated her birthday in March, but her birth certificate said January. Did that have something to do with the adoption?" Kurt asked.

"Yes. She was born in January, but my sister always celebrated her birthday on the day she got her. That was to make the people in Dallas believe it was her own."

"Did you ever tell Terri?" Cindy asked.

"No. There were many times my heart ached to tell her, but I always resisted because I didn't know what it would do to her relationship to my sister. My sister really needed her. But now . . . well, I wonder if I shouldn't have told her," Jan said, staring out of the window.

"I wonder what would have happened if you had kept her," Kurt said.

"You have to live with the thought that you didn't win her to Christ, but I have to live with that question," Jan said. "I thought I was doing what was best for her at the time, but now I wonder. The way her home life turned out, I wonder if I couldn't have done as much for her, even though she would not have known a father. It's something we will never know," Jan said.

They finished their dessert in silence, then Jan said, "I suppose you heard that Jim Hagen is in a drug rehabilitation center for treatment?"

"It's about time," Kurt muttered.

"You're still bitter, aren't you?" Jan said.

"Why shouldn't I be? Because of Jim and his drugs a lot of people have been hurt."

"I was bitter at first, too," Jan said. "I was angry at Jim and his drug pusher, and maybe even a little angry at God, but I've had to learn a lot about love in these last few weeks."

"Haven't we all," Kurt said under his breath.

"I had to ask God to help me see them as people for whom He died, rather than as killers. Not until then was I able to find peace."

"I'll accept them as persons," Kurt said, "but when I think of the heartache they caused all of us, it is hard to love them."

"That's something you will have to work through for yourself," Jan said. "Nobody can help you there."

The topic drifted to other things, and eventually they all went back to Jan's house. Jan invited them in, but because Cindy had to leave for camp again at 5:00 p.m, they decided not to accept her invitation.

As they were driving back to Kurt's place, Cindy said, "I don't know about you, but Jan sure convicted me today. I just can't see how she can be so forgiving . . . especially when I know now that Terri was her own daughter."

"Yeah, me, too," Kurt said. "I stood around Terri's casket and told God I would do anything He wanted me to do, and go anywhere He wanted me to go, and yet I get angry every time I even think about Jim. With that kind of attitude, it's going to be hard for God to use me."

"It's easy for me to love those kids at camp, but loving an enemy is something else," Cindy said.

Kurt suddenly pulled over to the curb. "You know what I want to do? I want to go see Jim right now. Maybe a visit at the drug center would show him that we do care about him, and the longer I wait to do it, the harder it will be."

"Are you sure you're ready for this?" Cindy asked.

"As ready as I'll ever be," Kurt answered. "I heard someone say that love had to start with an action. I don't feel any love for him right now, but I can show that I care."

"Do you know where the new center is located?"

"Sure. I drive by it every day on the way to work. Let's go."

So Kurt drove to the drug rehabilitation center which was located at the site of a veteran's hospital near the center of town. As he parked, Cindy asked, "Do you want me to go with you?"

"No, I need you to stay in the car and pray for me," he said.

Kurt got out, and with reluctant steps, approached the entrance. He was reminded of his visits to the hospital, but this time he was greeted by a man in a uniform at the reception desk.

"I wonder if I could see a patient, Jim Hagen?" Kurt asked.

The man looked on his list, and then said, "Follow me."

Kurt was led into a small conference room, and told to wait. In a few minutes the receptionist returned, followed by Jim.

"Well, you're the last person I expected to see here," Jim said.

"I don't blame you," Kurt said, "but I need to talk to you."

Jim sat down across from Kurt, and eyed him suspiciously. "So what do you want?"

"I really don't want anything," Kurt began. "I just heard you were here, and I wanted you to know I was thinking about you . . . and I'll be praying for you." Kurt was almost surprised to hear himself say those words.

"I never expected to hear that from you," Jim said.

"I still hurt a lot when I think of that Friday night, but God has used the experience to start a lot of us thinking . . . especially me," Kurt said.

"I've had a lot of time to think things over in here," Jim said. "My memories of that night aren't exactly pleasant either. I would give anything in the world if I could live that night over."

"Neither of us will be able to live it over, but we can make sure it doesn't happen again. There are a lot of things about that night that I should have done differently, too," Kurt said. "But I've changed a lot through all of this. If I hadn't changed, I wouldn't have been able to come here to talk to you."

"I guess you do have a good reason to hate me," Jim said. "I'm sorry about the beating . . . especially since I found out you didn't tip off the police that night of the party."

"How did you find that out?"

"Through the police and Chester. He's in jail, you know, and he's been doing a lot of talking— and implicating. He said he and Terri knew each other from Dallas. It seems he had been caught once before down there, and to get himself off the hook, he identified his customers . . . Terri was one of them."

"So that's why she was so frightened when she saw him at your party," Kurt said.

"Yeah, and she's the one who called the police after she got home. They identified her voice from the recording."

"But why did she tell you where I was going to be that night when you beat me up?" Kurt asked.

"She didn't. She had heard me talk about it,

so she knew something was coming, but didn't know when or where. We were just cruising around, saw your car at the hotel, and followed you home."

"And to think I blamed her for it," Kurt said.

"That's the way we wanted it," Jim said.

"That still doesn't answer why she would go into town with you and Chester that Friday night . . . especially if she hated him so," Kurt said.

"She didn't know Chester was in the car," Jim said. "He had hidden in the back so that the guards at the gate wouldn't see him. It wasn't until we were on the road that he sat up. When she saw him, she became so hysterical that she grabbed the wheel, and since I was in no condition to stop her, we crashed."

"That sure makes me feel better toward you," Kurt said. "Sorry about the way I talked to you in the hospital. There's still a lot about this drug culture I don't understand. For instance, I still don't really understand why Terri had to go with you that night."

"If you had ever been hooked on drugs, you'd understand. She hated them and everyone connected with them, yet couldn't control herself when she got desperate for them."

"I guess it takes someone bigger than ourselves to help break a habit like that," Kurt said.

"I'm trying. I hope this place can help me," Jim said.

"They can do a lot, but you need the extra help Christ can give. Could I come back and talk to you about Him?" Kurt asked.

"I can only have visitors twice a week, but I'll be glad to see you anytime," Jim said.

"How about next Sunday afternoon?"

"Sure. See you then."

They shook hands and Kurt turned to go.

"Thanks for coming," Jim called after him.

"Thanks for the information you gave me today. It makes me feel a lot better. See you Sunday."

They waved, and Kurt went out to the car where Cindy was waiting.

"From the look on your face, it must not have been too painful," Cindy said as Kurt slid into the driver's seat.

"I think I just found another reason for everything," Kurt said, his face beaming. "And I've just had a great lesson on love."

"Will you share it with me?" Cindy asked.

"Which? The lesson or love?"

"How about both?" Cindy answered as she slid over next to him.